Nell's Journeys in Australia...

PORT DOUGLAS

ALICE SPRINGS

AYERS ROCK
ULURU

SYDNEY

N
E
W
S

Nell in Australia · Nell's New Life

Dedication

This author dedicates this book to his Granddaughter, ELLEN SARAH, a Child of the Millennium, and All the Children of the Millennium, for whom this book is written and illustrated in the hope all you Children will grow up to love and honour the Sea and protect its Marine Life whether it be the majestic Whales of the Great Oceans or the tiny creatures on our beaches and in the little seaside rock pools.

The illustrator Ruth Bayley dedicates her artwork to the memory of her late husband, companion and colleague, David Coney.

This book belongs to

Nell of the Seas

BY MARK SCOTT
ILLUSTRATED BY RUTH BAYLEY

The Book Guild Limited

Sussex, England

Acknowledgements

The author is sincerely appreciative of the advice and assistance of Dr Eleanor Murray Steiner as Literary Consultant, whose love of Scotland and whose lifetime service and support for Highlanders and Islanders inspired this book.

Special thanks too to Mr Donald Murray, an ardent Gaelic Islander and retired headmaster of Dunning School near Gleneagles, Perthshire, who read the first draft and corrected my rudimentary Gaelic, for which I am responsible.

Also to my tutor of Marine Biology, Miss Terry Donovan BSc, and the University of Glasgow for teaching me that Marine Biology and Marine Conservation is an exciting lifetime discovery and study.

To my son Jan, my staunch sailing companion, whose steady hand on the helm of our boat has made our voyages around the islands such adventures.

P & O Cruises, whose happy liner voyages have taught me much about the world's oceans and faraway continents and tropical islands and in whose comfortable cabins this book was drafted.

Finally, these Nell stories could not reach the readers without the encouragement and professional expertise of Carol Biss, the Managing Director of The Book Guild, whose gentle but firm chiding ensured the manuscript was delivered timeously for her courteous and conscientious editorial and production team, Joanna Bentley and Janet Wrench, to publish. Ruth Bayley would like to show her appreciation of the co-operation and the assistance of Stephen Wheele and Claire Denyer of Viccari Wheele Ltd.

First published in Great Britain in 2002 by: The Book Guild Ltd, 25 High Street, Lewes, East Sussex BN7 2LU

Copyright © Mark Scott 2002

The right of Mark Scott to be identified as the author of this work has been asserted by him in accordance with the Copyright, Designs and Patents Act 1988.

Designed by Viccari Wheele Ltd
Designer: Claire Denyer

Origination, printing and binding in Singapore under the supervision of MRM Graphics Ltd, Winslow, Bucks.

A catalogue record for this book is available from The British Library.

ISBN 1 85776 680 6

Contents

4

Nell and the Old Man of the Seas

- Book One -

This is the tale of a lonesome little girl, Nell, who lives on a small remote island called Ellenabeich in the Atlantic, alongside the stormy west coast of Scotland where the west winds beat against the silver grey rocky shoreline.

This is the tale of a lonesome little girl, Nell, who lives on a small remote island called Ellenabeich in the Atlantic, alongside the stormy west coast of Scotland where the west winds beat against the silver grey rocky shoreline.

This is the edge of Scotland where the seabirds, seals and otters look westwards at dusk into the great orange globe of the setting sun far away towards Ireland and the Americas. This is the home of snow white and slate grey seagulls, who huddle on the high cliffs and glide like nature's kites into the gusty winds and hover or soar on the breezes just above the foam-tipped waves that dash on the blue-grey shingle beach. This is where tiny pink crabs the size of thumbnails hide beneath the long shiny bronze ribbons of kelp seaweed which

have been torn from the seabed by the rolling tides and where the little limpets cling inside their shell tents even tighter on the coastal rocks being scoured by the icy-blue sea.

This is what Nell sees when she awakens each morning and looks out from the bedroom window of her old granite house that has withstood the gales near the stormy oceanside for over a hundred years.

And this is what Nell was watching the wild night before her birthday on the 26th of January, when the stormy spring gale was wailing in the cold dusk outside.

Nell would be eight years old tomorrow. She was wanting a little West Highland terrier dog as a birthday present because she was sometimes ill and

7

lonely and wanted a pet to fondle and take walking on the beach and to romp with in the garden. Nell was kneeling by the window with her nose pressed against the cold glass on which her warm breath left misty circles below her nose. She was kneeling to pray for her birthday present dog which she had been asking her father for the past month to give her. She would call her puppy Westie (or Siarrach in Gaelic).

Nell could hear her mother, May, and her father, Jack, moving about and talking in the kitchen below, and she could smell the appetizing aroma of her mother's fresh home-made bread which her parents were having for their bedtime supper. She could hear her mother say to her father, 'But Jack! Who would look after a dog for Nell when you have gone away to Australia to

work?' Her mother had a soft kindly voice which seemed to match her soft brown hair.

'Don't worry, May,' her father was saying in his slow deep tones, with which he soothed Nell and her mother whenever they were troubled. 'Everything happens for a reason and in time all will be right in the end. Have no fear nor worries. Life will be good. Come along, it's late and time for us to sleep.'

Nell could hear them climbing the stairs and she scampered back into her own bed and pulled the blankets over her because she knew her mother and father always came to kiss her goodnight. After they came in and tucked her blankets around her they went to their own bedroom on the other side of the old house, where the wooden floors creaked as they trod.

Then the house was silent again, except for

9

the measured ticking of the old grandfather clock downstairs which was as tall as her father and older than her old grandfather. Gently Nell eased herself out from the envelope of warm blankets and moved to the window and knelt down again to look out to the sea. Outside, the gusts of cold north wind burst against the house and Nell shivered a little as she hugged herself to keep warm. The cold north wind had always been a part of her life.

It was almost dark outside now. The pale moon was high in the sky like a small piece of sliced lemon and the moonshine made the sea look as icy green as the melting icebergs in the Arctic north while the waves lapping the rocks below her window looked milky white.

Tomorrow was her birthday and she would stay awake to hear if her father had brought her birthday pet into the house in the morning. Nell put on her old brown woollen dressing-gown which made her look like a sack of potatoes as she knelt down again with her nose close to the window.

It was getting colder in her room as the north wind tapped against the window pane and cast pine needles from the fir tree beside the house against the glass. Outside the midnight moonlight looked frosty. The sheep on the hills in the distance above her house were lying still like snowballs in their white winter overcoats. All was still except for the waves which seemed to keep rhythm with the tick of the old clock which had been on the wall when her grandfather had been born in the last century.

Nell was very fond of her grandfather for the way he told her sea fables about the Sea Giant, Bodach Na Mara (which in English means the Old Man of the Seas), who sat on the rock outside the house and protected seamen and fisherfolk in times of storm and tempest. He told her that the old Sea Giant wrote down children's wishes and dreams on his oyster shells with a seagull's feather quill.

Nell's grandfather lived in a seaman's cottage at the nearby harbour and Nell watched his little white boat bobbing on its mooring in the bay, while two otters scrambled along the shingle into the dark green water and disappeared below the waves. When they surfaced they swam towards the big rock where, to her delight, she saw the Old Man of the Seas, the Bodach, sitting with his feet in the water, tugging shreds of seaweed out of his long white hair and beard. She had only seen the Old Man of the Seas once before when, as a very little girl long ago, her grandfather lifted her high on his shoulder in the garden so she could see over the wall to watch the Sea Giant. Nell knew that the Bodach could grant wishes because it was long ago that she wished a sea tempest would stop hurling the waves against the sea wall and that her house would not be washed away by the mighty waves.

Nell waved to the Old Man of the Seas sitting on the rock and he stopped combing his beard and waved back to her. So she closed her eyes and

made her birthday wish again. She asked for a little Scottish terrier dog which she would call Westie, and also that one day she would be able to go to Australia with her father and mother if she did not have the dog. When she opened her eyes she saw the Sea Giant waving farewell to her as he slid away from the big rock and disappeared into the dark waters, trailing ribbons of seaweed kelp behind him.

Nell scrambled back into bed and curled up under the warm blankets, still wearing her dressing gown. The midnight glow was growing dimmer. In a few hours her mother would call to Nell up the stairs and ring the little brass kitchen handbell to awaken Nell for breakfast. The little girl was growing sleepier and sleepier in the warm bed and she could not remain awake. So she fell deeply asleep into a dreamland where the Old Man of the Seas was with her father, who was holding a little white dog and her mother was fussing around her father and the dog and complaining that the Sea Giant was dripping water on her polished floor. And so Nell dreamed through the night until she heard the tinkle of the little brass bell to wake her for her breakfast porridge.

Up jumped Nell out of bed. She dressed quickly and scurried down the stairs to the kitchen, warmed by its big old cooker. Her father was sitting at the table in his dark blue seaman's jersey and his old peaked seaman's cap and he was enjoying his porridge and warm milk. Mother May was pouring more water into the big black porridge pot. But there was no dog... nowhere in the kitchen... nor was there any water spilt on Mother's polished floor. It had all been a dream for Nell.

'Happy Birthday, Nell,' her father greeted her.

'Happy Birthday, dear,' said Mother gently as she stroked Nell's cheek. Father patted Nell's shoulder and said, 'Put your shoes on, dear, we've got a surprise for you.' And he took her by the hand to the kitchen porch. There was a small rabbit hutch in the corner with a charming fluffy white rabbit inside, busily nibbling green leaves.

'That's Snowy - or Sneachda, as we say in Gaelic,' said Mother. Snowy had wide hazel eyes that melted away Nell's disappointment that Sneachda wasn't a white Highland terrier.

Nell tried to smile but her eyes were tearful.

'We are sorry, dear. We could not give you a little dog because Daddy cannot take a dog to Australia and we could not leave one here on the Island without you.'

Nell felt the tears tumbling down her cheek. 'But I wanted a little dog and I also want to go to Australia with you.'

Father was a tall strong fisherman whose hard leathery hands had hauled up fishing nets and lobster pots for many years to feed the Islanders. But now large fishing ships from foreign countries across the ocean had caught all the fish in the bay and had trawled the sea bed clear of shellfish and so her father was leaving Scotland to work as a seaman on the other side of the world where fish swam in the clear Australian waters.

'I know you wanted a dog but it's not practical now I am going away to Australia... so Snowy can now be your pet.' And Mother, who was always so sensible, added, 'A rabbit won't chase the sheep like a dog.'

'Will I be able to bring Snowy to Australia when I come to see you?' asked Nell. Father smiled and chuckled deeply like a rumble, and Mother explained, 'There are millions of rabbits in Australia already - and kangaroos. You can have a dog there.'

That made Nell happy and she stroked Snowy's ears before going back into the house to get ready for school.

Waiting for the school bus she was joined by her friend Tom who lived nearby. Tom was the local farmer's son and, wishing her 'Happy Birthday', he gave her his apple as a present. When she told him she did not get a dog but Snowy, Tom was pleased, because a dog would chase his father's sheep and frighten the otters in the bay. The otters were swimming in the bay as they spoke. Nell told him how she had seen Bodach Na Mara on the rock. Tom just laughed and shook his golden hair in the wind. He said Nell must have dreamt it. They were both laughing when the school bus arrived and all the children sang 'Happy Birthday' to Nell, who felt shy and blushed at being the centre of attention in the bus.

At school she asked her teacher Miss Murray about the Sea Giant and Miss Murray explained that the Bodach Na Mara was an ancient Gaelic mythical spirit who lived in olden times in the sea at the edge of the world and only came close to the coastline on moonlit nights and during storms to see what humans had done to the sea and coast.

'According to legend, ' said Miss Murray, ' the Old Man of the Seas had the power to grant a wish to anyone who respected the sea and who could pronounce the ancient Gaelic motto "Nach Uramach an Cuan", which means "How worthy of honour is the sea". The Old Man of the Seas expects humans to treat the sea and all its sea life with the same respect they show to their mother and father or to a child.'

'But I do respect the sea - I do not throw litter into the water and I do not damage the sea life,' protested Nell. 'I love the sea and the sea creatures.'

'Then,' said Miss Murray, who was a wise

old teacher, 'your wish shall be granted, but only when the time is right and you are ready for the gift.' She explained, 'It is the wisdom of the Old Man of the Seas to teach the children of the world to be thoughtful for nature on land and sea and to be patient in life because everything comes to those who wait and watch. The Sea Giant, or Bodach, honours those who honour the sea,' emphasized Miss Murray, and this is what Nell kept repeating to herself on the way home on the bus.

That night she kept her silent vigil at her bedroom window. The moonlight lay like a white bedsheet on the dark night-time sea. The sea rock throne of the old Sea Giant was empty and only a single seal played around the rock where a seagull was perched looking out to sea.

Nell was disappointed at the old Bodach's absence as she wanted to tell him her troubles. Tears ran down her cheeks and she put her cold hands on her face to cover her tears. When she took away her hands she was astonished to see old Bodach sitting there on his rocky outpost. The seagull was flying overhead and the seal was bobbing beneath the water by the Old Man's foot. The otters were no longer scurrying on the shoreline and all was quiet and still except the gentle rolling of the rhythmic waves.

The moon illuminated the Old Man's face and white beard when he turned to look at Nell at her window. She waved to him and signalled she would come but he waved her back. She put on her warmest dressing gown and her beach shoes and went downstairs to the garden which was only a short distance from the old Bodach's sea rock.

Nell was a sensible girl who had always heeded the advice and warnings of her grandparents and parents not to go out alone at night nor to go to the sea alone, especially after nightfall. The wise old Sea Giant does not want children near the water in the dark and he waved to Nell to stay behind her garden wall. She watched him stand up from the rock and slowly walk across the shingle beach towards her.

'Oh! Thank you for coming,' said Nell. She remembered Miss Murray's advice and added, 'I do respect the sea and my father respects the sea and all in it'. The Old Man nodded and replied, 'Yes, Ninag*, I know you do. I see what happens on the coasts, the beaches and inlets and bays and the seagulls tell me what they see. They call you "Child of the Wind"†. I know who does not damage the seas.'

The lights in the house went on as her father was putting logs on the fire to keep the home warm. Nell looked at the Old Man with the wet

* 'little girl' in English
† 'Leanabh na gaoith' in Gaelic

17

seaweed over his shoulders. He did not look cold standing there in the sea.

'Is it true you can grant wishes?' Nell asked him.

The old Bodach lifted his hand to his forehead and murmured, 'Wishes can only come true if they are so strong they can fly to the stars or ride the waves like a porpoise in a storm.'

Nell sighed and said, 'And what about dreams?'

'Well,' the Old Man said slowly and thoughtfully, 'dreams are like wishes. Everyone must have a wish or a dream, if they want to have a wish or a dream to come true. Everything anyone achieves, or any success they have, is a dream come true. And if you believe something strongly enough you can achieve it. We often become what we think and dream about. The only difference between a wish and a dream is whether you are awake or asleep. Everything always happens for a reason and in time we come to understand why.' The Old Man smiled at her. 'What is it you wish for, Ninag?' he asked.

Nell told him her father was going to Australia to help save the fish on the coral reefs and when her mother had found a house Nell wanted to join her parents in Australia, and go there with her grandmother on a big ship.

'That is both a wish and a dream and each can come true for you,' said the old Bodach. 'Your father is a very good seaman. He respects the sea and the sea life. In Australia he will prosper because there those who honour the sea are honoured and rewarded. He will be able to get a house for all of you because Australia is a land for families.'

Nell started jumping up and down with excitement, especially when the old Bodach added,

'You will have your next birthday in Australia, if you honour your parents and grandparents. Until then you must learn all that you can about the sea and sea life because the world must do more to protect the sea.'

Nell was not sure what all that meant and she was silent while she thought of all the lessons at school and the knowledge that her parents and grandfather had given her, such as their sea lore and wisdom.

Suddenly the house door opened and Father shouted, 'What are you doing out there, Nell? Come back into the house and out of the wind right away.'

Nell waved goodbye to the Old Man and ran back to the house. Ancient Bodach slipped away into the sea saying, 'Farewell, Leanabh na gaoith,' and was gone away with the tide to another ocean far away from Scotland.

Child of the Wind

- Book Two -

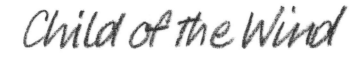

The Story of Nell's Voyage to Australia

We left Nell and the Old Man of the Seas, the Bodach, on the rocks outside her island home on a stormy day. The Bodach slipped away into the sea saying, 'Farewell, Child of the Wind,' and he disappeared with the tide to reach another ocean far away.

Our next story tells how Nell and her grandmother leave their island home to travel on an adventurous voyage to the other side of the world on a cruise ship. They sail across the wide oceans of the world in stormy seas over the Equator to the tropical sun. They visit marvellous distant continents and enjoy exciting adventures in different lands.

CHAPTER ONE

Ship Ahoy! Around the World

The Inner Hebridean islands off the west coast of Scotland are storm-battered by the wintry south-west gales each November, when the autumn storms force the fishermen to tie up their boats on the shores and keep the islanders inside their cosy fishermen's cottages or farmhouses.

The nightfall dusk descends early as the winter cold chills the land and sea alike. The dark ink-blue night sky only slowly turns misty grey when morning dawns and the sun is still not bright enough to warm the sea and the land.

One winter morning on the Island, Nell was standing at the window of her weather-beaten old stone house, looking at the dull dawn light as the waves were dashing and crashing against the rocks at the end of the garden. She peered into the mist that was like a veil on the mainland beyond the harbour where her grandfather's ferry boat was moored to the jetty. Behind her on her bedroom walls were pinned colourful postcards of sunny, golden Australia, sent to her by her mother and father, who had emigrated to Australia a few months earlier.

Her father, Jack, had been a fisherman on the island like his father, grandfather, and ancestors before him. Jack and Grandfather worked hard from early in the mornings until late nightfall, but now there were not enough fish left to catch to earn a living to support the family. So Father went to Australia to work as a seaman with a Sea Life Protection unit on Queensland's Great Barrier Reef, which is made of coral and is home for all kinds of sea life. The Reef is the world's largest living creature and is the eighth natural wonder of the world.

Nell's mother, May, had also gone out with her father to Queensland to help him find a new home for Nell and her grandparents, who would also go to Australia and be a family again.

As Nell watched the ice-green cold Atlantic waters of the sea of the Hebrides outside her shoreline house, downstairs in the warm kitchen,

Grandmother was tinkling the little brass handbell to call Nell and Grandfather for the breakfast porridge.

As the three were enjoying the warm milky oatmeal, the Island postman, called 'Hamish the Post', knocked on the kitchen window and shouted, 'Guid marnin', Nell! Here's another letter from Australia.' Nell jumped up from the breakfast table and ran to the door to collect the thick envelope with its beautiful stamps showing colourful pictures of Australian animals and fish. But she couldn't open the letter because it was addressed in her mother's graceful handwriting to Grandmother, to 'Mrs Anderson and Family'. Nell gave the letter to Grandmother.

'Please, Grandma, read it aloud.' Grandmother put on her silver rimmed spectacles and took several pages and two large, official, important tickets from the envelope. Grandma was smiling with pleasure, and even stern old Grandfather was looking excitedly at the two large tickets.

Grandma adjusted her spectacles. 'We had all better sit down - it's a long letter,' she said in Gaelic in the serious voice she used whenever she spoke in Gaelic instead of English.

Grandma then explained that Mother's letter reported that Father enjoyed his work on the coral reef conservation and that Mother had set up home in a nice little wooden bungalow in Port Douglas

near the Four Mile Beach and that the house was ready for Nell and Grandmother. So the two large tickets were for Nell and Grandma to travel on the Pacific and Orient, the P & O cruise liner *Arcadia*, to Australia. When her parents could afford the money to buy a ticket for Grandfather he could join them later.

Grandfather looked solemn. 'I understand,' he said. 'It costs a lot of money to go to Australia. I can't go now in any event because I must stay behind to look after the Island boats and keep the ferry going to take the folk to Oban. And I will also look after Snowy for you.'

'Oh, Grandpa!' said Nell. 'We can't leave you behind on your own.'

The old mariner looked at her with kindly blue eyes.

'Don't worry, Nell,' he said, 'I'll be all right meantime.'

Grandma then took off her spectacles, pushed up her sleeves and said she would have to start thinking about packing the cases for the long voyage in January.

A few days later the P & O Shipping Company sent Grandma a large package with what was called an information pack about the ship and a map of the voyage as well as luggage labels for all their baggage.

With all the excitement of planning for the 14,651-mile long voyage and Nell studying the world atlas beside Grandfather, who had sailed the Seven Seas when he was a young seafarer, the sailing departure date soon came. So Nell and her grandparents travelled across the famous Bridge over the Atlantic which connects Ellenabeich to the mainland and on to Oban. There they boarded the train to travel through Scotland and England to Southampton to join the good ship *Arcadia* that would take Nell and Grandma thousands of miles to the other side of the world.

Atlantic Bridge

CHAPTER TWO

A Floating Palace

Grandma was pleased she was travelling by cruise liner instead of aeroplane because she said she didn't like heights and only birds were meant to fly. Grandfather just smiled whenever Grandma Anderson talked about aeroplanes, birds and people not having wings.

He smiled even more with pleasure and amazement when he saw the huge glistening white luxury cruise ship moored at Southampton Docks. It was all so different from when Grandpa had been a young sailor on an old coal steamer that sailed from Southampton to Australia with Scottish machinery. That was half a century ago, before Nell's parents were even born, and it took several months to make the voyage then. Hundreds of people were boarding the *Arcadia*, which looked like a stately white-walled castle and would be their floating home for the next few weeks. It was all very modern and shiny.

After the excitement and the farewells to Grandfather, Grandma and Nell also boarded the great liner, where a ship's steward took the little girl and the old lady to their cabin. There were eleven storeys - or decks - on the ship and they travelled up and down in a lift. Every time the lift stopped at one of the decks a strange recorded voice told the passengers, 'Mind the doors, please. Mind the doors.' Eventually, the steward stopped the lift to take them to their cabin at the end of a long corridor, which was even longer than Nell's school corridor.

When the cabin door was opened Grandma gasped with astonishment - it was just like a de luxe hotel room with two beds, a writing desk, a shower and a television. Nell thought most important of all was the large window with a wide ledge, on which she could sit and look out at the water just a few feet below the strong thick glass.

'We're awfully close to the sea!' exclaimed Grandma, who took one look out of the window and then went back to explore all the cabin cupboards. 'We've even got a telephone and a fridge with fruit juices in it,' she said. 'And a world atlas and a ship's newsletter to keep us informed. Just imagine, Nell, this will be our home for the next six weeks.'

There was a knock on the cabin door and the steward was standing there with a tea tray and biscuits and cake. He asked them if he could help them unpack their luggage. Grandma said he was very kind and asked his name. He said he was Luiz and he was from Goa in India, which seemed right to Nell because he had a wonderful sun tan just like the waiters at the Indian Saifoor restaurant in

Oban where Grandma had taken her for a curry while waiting for the train. Luiz was a friendly man whose black shiny hair completely contrasted to Grandma's white braids. He was surprised when Grandma told him they came from Scotland because he said she and Nell both spoke very good English.

'Of course we do. And we speak Gaelic as well,' which impressed Luiz, who said he had never been to Scotland but he had heard it was a cold and windy country with icy seas.

'Of course it is,' said Nell. 'That's why I'm called the Child of the Wind.' Luiz looked even more impressed and repeated, 'Child of the Wind. That's lovely.'

Grandma walked over to the window and looked concerned. 'Does the sea ever come up to the window?' she asked Luiz. His smile widened.

'No, no, no, Madam,' he was anxious to reassure her. 'And the window doesn't open either, so don't worry about forgetting to close it. That's why each cabin has air-conditioning to keep you cool in the tropics and warm in the cold climates.'

Luiz told them he would return later to take them to the Dining Room for the evening dinner.

CHAPTER THREE

The Big Feast

In the Dining Room, Nell had never seen so many people in one place - even more than went to the annual Highland Games back home on her Island, and they were not all of the 1400 passengers. There were so many diners that two separate sittings for dinner were necessary. Nell and Grandma went to the first sitting.

It seemed to Nell that she was the only little girl there, but the ship was so big and with more than a thousand passengers there might be another little girl or boy somewhere aboard this floating township.

The steward informed Nell and her grandmother that there was a Swiss boy called Jan sitting at the next table. He was a golden-haired boy with blue eyes and an impish smile and when he noticed Nell looking at him he waved to her and Grandma in a friendly gesture of greeting. He was about 10 years old and was sitting with his parents.

At their dining table Luiz introduced them to their two table waiters, Alvin and Alex, who were also Indians from Goa. Their other table companions introduced themselves. Nell sat in the middle of one side of the table and Grandma sat next to her on the left. On the right of Nell was an English lady called Miss Rachel Leigh who had a gentle smile, so Nell liked her immediately, especially when Miss Leigh said, 'I think Nell is a beautiful name. I like your kilt. What is the tartan?' So Nell happily told her it was the Anderson tartan. Nell knew they were going to be good friends. Later Nell learned that Miss Leigh was an artist who knew the names of all the colours.

The man who sat directly opposite Nell looked very serious. He was a thoughtful American, Mr Stone, with a bushy moustache and large grey eyes, who peered through his spectacles as if he was trying to see and remember all the hustle and bustle of what was happening. On his

left-hand side was Dr Janet Thompson, an Australian marine biologist who was returning home to Queensland after working in Europe. She looked very clever and she was cheerful and chatty to the lady artist Miss Leigh and Mr Stone.

On the other side of Mr Stone opposite Grandma was another elderly lady, Mrs Pearson, who was returning to her Australian home in Perth after visiting her son in London. She was a retired school teacher who reminded Nell a little bit of her Island school teacher Miss Murray, but whose Australian accent was completely different from Miss Murray's soft Scottish voice.

Nell had never heard so many questions or seen so many people of different nationalities in one place before. So she was relieved when the waiters gave the large menu cards to each adult, who immediately began studying the delicious selection of dishes. The waiters asked Nell if she wanted the children's menu with a variety of special puddings and ice creams but Nell politely replied that she was eight years old and could read very well.

Unfortunately, when Nell started reading the menu there were a lot of French words she did not understand, like consommé, hors d'oeuvres and strange desserts liked Baked Alaska, Gateaux, Peach Melba and Pavlova. But there was not a mention of custard or rice pudding. Luckily the kindly Miss Leigh explained the menu to her. Nell thought it took as long to read the menu as to eat the meal, but at least she and Grandma would not need to wash the dishes when the four-course meal was over.

Everyone said they had travelled a long way to join the ship at Southampton and, after such a large feast, they all said they were wanting to go to their cabins to sleep so they could be awake when the ship cast off its moorings in the morning to start their world cruise.

'So, off to bed, Nell,' said Grandma. They left the Dining Room and walked down the long corridors to the lift to take them to their cabin. Inside, Nell selected the bed nearest the window. It was very dark outside now, except for the harbour lights. She and Grandma were soon fast asleep.

CHAPTER FOUR

Exploring the Ship

When Nell awoke, the little clock on the cabin table showed it was six o'clock in the morning, and Grandma was still sound asleep. So Nell crept out of bed and looked out of the window. To her amazement she saw the water outside rushing past the glass. The ship was moving! The white sea spray was splashing the glass.

'Grandma! Grandma!' squealed Nell. 'We're moving! We're moving!'

Grandma slowly awakened and sleepily shook her head.

'Are you sure, Nell? It doesn't feel as if we are moving.' Grandma put on her dressing gown and looked out of the window. 'Gracious me!' she said, as she peered through the glass at the grey dawn sky and the white-topped waves splashing the window. 'I never felt us moving. We must have been asleep when we left the harbour so quietly and smoothly that it didn't even awaken us.' She was shaking her head in disbelief at it all.

Grandma rang for cabin service on the cabin telephone and when Luiz, the cabin steward, arrived he informed them they could have breakfast in their cabin or in the self-service buffet on the Lido deck. They decided it would be more exciting to go to the buffet. When they arrived there a couple of hundred other passengers were already enjoying a selection of English cooked breakfast, French croissants, Canadian pancakes and maple syrup and even Scottish porridge.

While everyone was enjoying the meal, they could look out through the observation windows as the stately liner cruised steadily down the English Channel on the first leg of her world voyage.

Nell had read the adventures of great explorers like Sir Walter Raleigh, Captain Cook and yachtswomen Clare Francis and Ellen MacArthur. But Nell had never imagined that she would also sail to the other side of the world and follow in the wake of pirates, buccaneers and the tea clippers to

Asia, or the convicts and prisoners who were transported from Scotland to Australia for stealing a sheep or a salmon.

The English Channel was quite calm, unlike Nell's Scottish Atlantic sea, and the west-south-west wind was mild, unlike the gales around Nell's Island. Nevertheless, even in calm seas there was a lifeboat drill, which Nell thought was exciting but Grandma thought was a bother.

Arcadia steamed onwards so steadily that Grandma decided they should walk along the promenade deck and explore the ship before they sailed out of the Channel and towards the usually stormy Bay of Biscay on their way to the first stop at Madeira, an island off the north west coast of Africa. They took the lift up past the various decks where they saw three swimming pools, a children's paddling pool, three restaurants, a cinema, a theatre, a library and six shops, a hairdressers and a gym and deck sports area.

It all took so long to explore that twice they had to stop and rest for milkshakes in the ice cream parlour and in the conservatory for morning coffee and biscuits before returning to their cabin to rest before lunch. Grandma was exhausted and

described *Arcadia* as more like a grand hotel than a ship - but Grandma had only travelled around the Scottish Islands on a small ferry and she had not been on such a great liner before.

After lunch they went to the sun deck with its panoramic views of the sea and the other ships and liners in the shipping lanes and sea routes on their voyages around the world. The English Channel is a highway to the world. Sailing ships in bygone centuries had navigated the Seven Seas from Britain to the five continents of South and North America, Africa and the Far East lands of China and Japan, and even further to Oceania for Australia and New Zealand.

On *Arcadia* the sun deck was buzzing with conversation as Grandma sat in a deck chair playing what she called her 'Passenger Watching Game'. Nell had never seen so many people of different nationalities, nor heard so many different languages spoken by the pale-looking Europeans, the colourfully-dressed Asians with their red and green robes, the smartly suited Japanese and Chinese, and the Americans and Canadians in their track suits.

CHAPTER FIVE

On the High Seas

As the ship left the English Channel and steamed closer to the Bay of Biscay, the weather worsened with a cold gale and the sea swell looked even taller than Nell, making the sea look angry just like back in the Hebrides. As this made the ship roll gently, many of the passengers left the top decks and returned to their cabins to rest and avoid seasickness.

But Nell and Grandmother were seasoned sailors and had been in much rougher seas off Scotland. They were chatting together in Gaelic about the voyage when the lady artist Miss Leigh joined them. She was very curious about Scotland, and their life on the Island, and the Gaelic language. Miss Leigh was such a natural, polite listener. She nodded interestedly as Nell explained about their family's Island home, about their Gaelic community and the ancient Gaelic tradition of 'Nach Uramach an Cuan', which means 'How worthy of honour is the sea'. Nell was so busy talking that Grandma closed her eyes and nodded into a snooze while Miss Leigh was wide-eyed in wonderment at the stories of ancient Gaelic traditions, especially Bodach Na Mara, who had called Nell 'Leanabh na gaoith'.

'It is Gaelic for Child of the Wind,' explained Nell.

'I shall call you Nell, the Child of the Wind,' said Miss Leigh. She explained that she was travelling to Australia to make sketches and paintings for children's school books and for the Australian tourist board. Nell had never met a real artist before, and she was fascinated by Miss Leigh's hold-all canvas bag with its sketch books, pencils and paints.

Then there was an announcement on the ship's loudspeaker system, which awakened Grandma, who shook her head and said, 'Good gracious! I fell asleep because the ship is rolling like a rocking chair.'

Bodach na Mara . . .

CHAPTER SIX

The Captain's Party

The announcement said that the ship's Captain would be welcoming all the passengers at a formal reception that evening in the ship's atrium, which was the hub of the ship's social life.

Grandma and Miss Leigh both agreed that everyone should wear their best dresses for such a formal occasion and off they hurried back to their cabins to prepare for the evening gathering.

With Grandma helping Nell, they both braided their hair with Anderson tartan ribbons and put on their best full length Anderson tartan dresses. They looked very elegant as they walked slowly down the stairs to the atrium. It seemed to Nell that everyone there was watching her and Grandma, but she was not embarrassed, just proud of herself: 'Nell of the Hebrides, the Child of the Wind'. Grandma looked to Nell like the Queen of the Scots, so she clutched Grandma's hand with pride. She also noticed that the Swiss boy Jan was very smartly dressed in his lederhosen: leather trousers with braces decorated with Alpine flowers and a little black, white and red skull cap like an Alpine climber.

When the large assembly of passengers was congregated, Captain Smith arrived, escorted by his assistant officers. He was dressed in a splendid snow white uniform and a peaked cap, all with gold braid just like an Admiral of the Fleet back in Scotland. He told them about the ship and the voyage and explained that the first rule of the sea was the safety of the ship and all those aboard, especially the women and children, which made Nell feel very secure in such a strong ship with a clever Captain and crew.

The Captain then explained that while he and his crew would care for the passengers, everyone on the liner had a duty to care for the sea and not damage the oceans with oil spills and rubbish or waste, and that nothing at all was ever to be thrown overboard from the ship into the sea, not even orange peel nor sweet papers.

'If we care for the sea, it will care for us,' said the Captain, and Nell thought he looked and sounded just like her Bodach Na Mara at home.

Grandma said she wished Grandpa was here to listen to the Captain's sea tales and adventures and to hear about how they would see whales, porpoises, sharks and flying fish in the oceans, and in the skies were giant albatross birds that circled the world soaring with the winds, as well as seagulls and terns flying around the Equator. The Captain also told them how they would drop anchor off different lands and islands, and meet interesting local peoples, islanders and tribesmen, and that it was important that the local customs and traditions be politely respected.

Everyone cheered and applauded the Captain and his officers when he had finished. On his way out he saw Nell and stopped to speak to her.

'Good evening, young lady,' he said in his deep voice behind his thick beard like Grandfather's. 'Welcome aboard. Have a good voyage!' He smiled at her and Grandma, and shook Grandma's hand.

'Excuse me, Sir,' said Nell, 'but who is steering the ship now you are here?' Captain Smith smiled even more.

'Well, young lady, we have a navigator and a helmsman while I am here, so don't you worry.' And off he went to see if the navigator was steering the right course.

Nell had never been called 'young lady' before and she felt very grown up. Usually people called her 'little girl' or, in Scotland, 'wee lassie', so she was very proud when the Captain spoke to her so graciously, and she was glad someone was steering the ship when the Captain was busy with his other duties.

As they went into the Dining Room everyone agreed that the Captain and all the crew made *Arcadia* a safe and happy ship. The huge Dining Room was brightly lit by chandeliers and wall lamps, with candle-lit tables. There were hundreds of people at the rows and rows of dining tables, each with smart black and white-dressed waiters. The lady passengers were wearing fashionable dresses and the gentlemen were in formal evening suits. Nell had only ever before seen such a scene on the television or in films.

CHAPTER SEVEN

Nell's New Friends

Nell was learning much by listening to all the unusual passengers and crew whom she and Grandma met when exploring the ship. There were also interesting lectures and talks about the places they would visit and a ship's library with fascinating books for Nell to read at night in the cabin while Grandma was sitting up in bed reading geography books and an atlas to follow the ship's course.

Before Nell left home, Grandpa had given her what he called a log-book, which was like a diary for her to write notes each day of what she did or saw and who she met. So each night Nell wrote a daily report in the log-book just as if she

Today I saw a lot of flying fish and a whale. It is very hot and I

was talking to Grandpa about her adventures and experiences.

The first stop on the voyage was the island of Madeira - four days after departing from England. So Nell began reading a library book about Madeira, which stands alone in the ocean off the north west coast of Africa. Although they were sailing closer to Africa, the weather remained cold, the wind became stronger and the sea swell was rising and falling three to four metres, or twelve feet - higher than a bus. Outside the ship there was a steady rainfall. The ship alternately rolled from side to side or pitched up and down like a roller coaster. Some passengers, like the Swiss boy Jan, from the big cities like London, Paris, Brussels and Zurich, who were not used to the sea and sailing, became seasick and remained in their cabins on their bunks, or visited the ship's doctors and nurses in the ship's hospital for seasickness tablets.

Because Nell and Grandma were used to sailing on Grandpa's ferry in the rough Scottish seas they were not seasick. Grandpa had taught them to relax at sea and not fight the ocean, and not to struggle against the rolling and pitching of a ship.

As the weather became cooler and the sea rougher, Nell and Grandma stayed in their warm cabin to read about Madeira. They had arranged with the ship's tour guide that they would go on a one-day tour of the island when they arrived there. Nell had never heard of Madeira before the cruise except for the home-made Madeira cake that Grandma often served with the family's afternoon tea.

As the liner neared Madeira in the early morning the island seemed small, but all the skyscraper hotels made the island look tall. When the ship moored alongside the pier, the liner looked as large as some of the multi-storey hotels on the island.

CHAPTER EIGHT

Madeira Island

A coach was on the dockside to take Nell, Grandma and some of the other passengers on a tour of the town of Funchal, the capital city, up the mountain slopes covered with sub-tropical flowers. They had only travelled a short distance when Nell was surprised by the fields of Christmas plants, the green and red poinsettias which were just like Grandma's Christmas plant at home, but these were giant size.

Jan sat on the bus seat next to Nell and he showed her his telescope and Swiss knife, and Nell showed him her sketch book. They spoke in English and also exchanged some words in Gaelic and German or French.

The coach took them up the steep winding road past the colourful little painted houses with thatched roofs, past the grape vineyards and banana plantations as well as the mimosa plants and willow trees from which the villagers shape their famous wickerwork baskets.

On the coach trip to the top of the mountain village of Santo de Serra the steep road made Grandma feel giddy because of the height, but she soon felt better when she saw the fields of Arum lilies and red and yellow flowers and herbs for making medicines. At the village the local people, who wore colourful hats and shawls, came with trinkets and basketware to sell when the coach stopped for afternoon tea. From the picturesque village, 2,000 feet above the sea, *Arcadia* appeared like a toy boat in the harbour.

Grandma and all the ladies hurried into the restaurant where Grandma chose a glass of Madeira wine and cakes. Nell requested a glass of sweet grape juice and a slice of Madeira cake, which the manager said his grandmother had made. But his Madeira cake didn't look nor taste like Grandma's afternoon tea Madeira cake back home.

'That's because my Scottish Madeira cake is made from a different recipe from this Madeira Madeira cake,' explained Grandma. When the manager heard this he said he would give Grandma his grandmother's recipe for Madeira Madeira cake if Grandma would give him her recipe for Scottish Madeira cake. Everyone gathered around the table while Grandma and the manager exchanged recipes and the coach driver lifted Nell up so she could see what was happening.

The manager was so pleased to get Grandma's recipe that he gave Grandma a whole freshly baked Madeira Madeira cake, which was so big that Grandma bought a large Madeira wicker basket from a little village boy to carry it back to the ship. Jan was so pleased when Grandma gave him a slice of the cake that he offered to carry the basket for her back to the ship. And he so enjoyed himself that he asked Grandma and Nell if he could go with them on their next tour ashore, which Grandma said was very nice but Nell was not so sure.

Everyone was happy and still laughing about Grandma's trophy on the bus back to the ship where, for the next week, Grandma and Nell ate

slices of the Madeira Madeira cake with their
afternoon tea in the cabin. Then Grandma
graciously wrote a letter to the manager of the
island restaurant thanking him and asking him to
compliment his grandmother on her excellent
Madeira cake. When Nell told everyone at the
dining table that evening about her adventure with
Grandma at Santo de Serra they all clapped hands
and said they would like to go with Grandma the
next time she went ashore for a trip.

CHAPTER NINE

Pirates and Treasure Island

After the ship slipped its moorings and left the island they were soon steering full steam ahead across the high seas, across the Atlantic Ocean towards the Caribbean Sea and the island of Tortola, the main island of the 40 British Virgin Islands which grow sugar cane, sweet potatoes, avocados, bananas, mangoes and other fruit. Long ago it was an island hideaway for buccaneers and pirates.

Mr Stone explained that Christopher Columbus had sailed to Tortola 500 years earlier

and that another one of the British Virgin Islands had inspired Robert Louis Stevenson to write the book *Treasure Island*, which Nell had read at school.

Dr Thompson said Tortola is famous for its white sandy beaches and turquoise sea and she said there was a strict conservation policy on the island. She promised to teach Nell how to see the sea life with a 'goggle box' - a plastic bucket with a glass bottom which you could put in the water and see the sea bottom and the fish swimming about the coral.

Nell couldn't get there fast enough and she asked Luiz if he could speak to the Captain to make the ship go faster. Luiz shook his head.

'No, no, Miss Nell,' he said, 'our Captain knows best. We are already going 20 knots, that's over 20 miles per hour. Leave it all to Captain Smith. Just like you leave it all to your Grandfather to skipper his ferry back home.'

Mrs Pearson looked puzzled so Nell explained to her that a knot is a nautical mile, which is 6,080 feet long, while a land mile is 5,280 feet long! It was the first time Nell had ever

taught something to a teacher and she was proud of herself.

Grandma nodded in agreement. 'You are quite right, Luiz,' she said, 'the Captain always knows best - just like Grandpa. They like to travel safely rather than quickly.' In fact, a lot of times on the voyage, many passengers wished the ship would go slower so they could see more things for longer.

While they were in the mid-Atlantic Ocean they did not see any land nor other ships and after they cruised further south the sun became brighter and hotter than the hottest Scottish summer day. So all the passengers who were lying on the sun deck lounger beds had to wear straw hats and sunblock to prevent sunburn. So did Nell, who enjoyed the swimming and paddling pools.

Nell and Jan were also taught how to play table tennis by a nice lady called Mrs Marion Phillips from Guernsey, who was the best player on the ship, but who was very strict about the rules of the game. When Jan batted the ping pong ball into the ship's swimming pool for Nell to get, Mrs Phillips insisted he jumped into the water to retrieve it. So he didn't do it often after that.

For three days they cruised under the tropical sun. Grandma enjoyed looking over the side of the ship from the promenade deck with Nell, watching the fairylike flying fish skim above the gently rolling sea beside the ship. They were joined by other passengers to watch the display of the silver fish that resembled giant dragonflies.

The marine biologist, Dr Thompson, joined Nell and explained that as the ship travelled further south towards the Equator they would see dolphins, sharks, whales and giant turtles as well as frigate birds and fairy terns and booby birds.

She also explained that as the ship travelled further southwards it was necessary to put back the clocks and watches by an hour, and that they were already four hours behind the time back home in Britain, so that when they were having lunch at twelve noon, Grandpa in Scotland would be having afternoon tea at four o'clock.

'The simple reason for all this,' said Dr Thompson, 'is the way the earth turns from west to east, making the sun appear to travel from east to west. We are travelling westwards on this ship.'

Later in the cabin Nell tried to explain it all to Grandma, who said she was not going to change the hands on her watch or the cabin alarm clock and she would keep Greenwich Mean Time and watch the ship's clocks instead for the local time wherever they were. Nell thought it would be very confusing to have two sets of clocks and watches.

CHAPTER TEN

Table Talk

That night at dinner the table companions discussed the adjustment of the clocks and also their daytime adventures.

Mr Stone, the writer, liked asking questions and Nell felt he remembered what people said. He always had a pencil in his coat pocket and he scribbled notes at the table on the ship's menu, which upset the waiters. Once he dropped his pencil in his soup!

Mr Stone was a world traveller and entertained the other passengers with his stories of the sea and seafarers. He and Dr Thompson liked exchanging information about the oceans and sea life.

Grandma, Miss Leigh and Mrs Pearson all listened politely and enjoyed their meals while Nell asked questions that the adults were too embarrassed to ask, like: Why is the sea salty? Why do the tides ebb and flow? Why are there different fish in the different oceans? What is the difference between a ship, a boat and a vessel or craft?

When Nell asked Mr Stone if he had ever seen the Bodach, the Sea Spirit, the old writer paused and doodled his pencil on the menu. He said that when he was a boy his grandfather, who had been a Scottish mariner, had read to him the legend of the Bodach.

'I grew up in a small fishing village in Florida, Nell. There my grandfather and his fellow seafarers respected the sea. You know, we need to respect the sea even more now than ever before because the sea is more important to mankind that it has ever been. The legend of the Bodach is just as important now as it was when I was a boy sixty years ago.'

Everyone at the table agreed except Mrs Pearson, who said she had never heard of the Bodach. She said the legend all sounded as strange as the legend of Scotland's Loch Ness Monster. She shrugged her shoulders and said she didn't believe in folk tales.

But Dr Thompson surprised them all: 'I'm

sorry to interrupt, Mrs Pearson, but the legend of the Bodach and the tradition of Uramach an Cuan expresses the respect for the sea and marine life by all the sea-going peoples of the world, including those in South America, Africa and Asia, not just the north lands of Europe.'

'I hope that's true, Dr Thompson,' said Miss Leigh, the artist. 'And I hope we can all agree that marine conservation is too important to argue about. We don't want any disagreements at the dining table to cause indigestion.'

Mrs Pearson slowly nodded agreement and said she understood some of the things said by Mr Stone and Dr Thompson. 'But I've never seen the Bodach, so I can't say whether I believe in him or not!' she said.

Mr Stone laughed. 'I've never seen China, but I know China is there. I've never seen the Loch Ness Monster, but I believe a mysterious creature does live in that silent deep loch.'

Mrs Pearson liked talking most about Australia because she had not travelled overseas before, and she taught Australian history to Australian children. She and Grandma became close friends. Grandma knew very little about Australia and she enjoyed Mrs Pearson's tales of kangaroos, koala bears and the mysteries of the Australian deserts or the Outback, which the old teacher liked more than the sea, that made her seasick.

The elderly American writer reminded the teacher that the Aboriginal people believed in the Dreamtime Spirit of the Outback. She agreed and admitted she found the Bodach sea legend was different but as interesting as the Aboriginal legends.

Grandma and Mrs Pearson were both very occupied in needlework and embroidery and they preferred discussing crochet or petit point. They also liked attending the ship's needlework classes and concerts.

The writer, Mr Stone, the scientist, Dr Thompson, and the artist, Miss Leigh, all enjoyed exchanging stories and folklore of the sea, and Nell was fascinated with them. Nell also enjoyed exploring the ship with Dr Thompson and Miss Leigh while Grandma and Mrs Pearson preferred their afternoon siesta when they fell asleep over their knitting or needlework on the sun loungers on the promenade deck.

CHAPTER ELEVEN

Nell's Special Friends

The thoughtful, observant artist was like Nell's mother. She said she preferred to be called Rachel, rather than Miss Leigh. The scientist preferred to be called Janet instead of Dr Thompson. Grandma liked them both to escort Nell about the ship while she rested, so Nell was never lonely.

Nell had never had an aunt and now it appeared she had two interesting aunts as well as Grandma. Both her adopted aunts liked swimming in the ship's heated pools, one of which was of sea-water and the other fresh water. Both were very warm, with water of 84°F in the hot tropical sun. The two ladies were surprised at how well Nell could swim and they all jumped into the pool water, which gently rolled like the waves with the rolling motion of the ship.

Grandma enjoyed watching from the sun deck but would not join them in the pool, nor would Mrs Pearson because they thought it was too deep, although Nell could stand up in the pool safely. Everyone suspected that the Australian teacher could not swim well but would not admit it because all Australians are expected to be excellent swimmers.

When the ship's pool attendant heard what Grandma and Mrs Pearson had said he gave the two ladies buoyancy rings and swimming armbands and then both elderly ladies joined Nell, Rachel and Janet in the pool. If Grandfather, Father and Mother could see how Nell held Grandma's hand in the pool and floated in the warm water, how proud they would be.

More and more people enjoyed swimming as the ship continued southwards closer to the Equator into the Caribbean Sea. The Swiss boy Jan sometimes came with his mother to the pool. He was not as good a swimmer as Nell but he enjoyed splashing about trying to compete with Nell, who had learned to swim in her local Atlantis Leisure Centre. Grandma liked Jan very much because he was very polite, and his mother and Grandma

flopped into the water like a walrus. She spoke sharply to Nell in a language which Nell did not understand. The woman then said in poor English that she and Jan should not be with adults in the swimming pool but in the children's paddling pool. Jan replied to her in her own language and politely told her that he was with his mother and they were allowed in the pool by the attendants.

The next day when the same thing happened, Jan dropped something into the pool near the woman, who he called Madame Walrus. Suddenly the large lady gave a yell and began clambering out of the pool, pointing to an object in the water. The pool attendant immediately retrieved a bright green plastic frog, which he showed to the angry lady, who pointed to the figure of Jan disappearing into the next pool.

Everyone laughed except Madame Walrus, who walked back to her deck chair and sat down on what appeared to be a large black spider but was another one of the boy's plastic imitations. She never spoke rudely to Nell nor Jan again, but always watched them suspiciously whenever she saw Jan.

enjoyed talking about this Swiss lady's crochet and lace work. Although he was polite to Grandma, he was a mischievous boy who enjoyed playing practical tricks.

One day when Nell and Jan were swimming, a large lady clambered into the pool and

CHAPTER TWELVE

Sailing to the Sun

It rarely rained on the voyage southwards but beautiful rainbows sometimes cast a brilliant arch over the sea and it seemed to Nell that the great liner would sail directly beneath the bridge of colour.

Fortunately Janet, the scientist, was there with Rachel, the artist, and Janet explained how rainbows formed while Rachel busily sketched the scene and transformed the colours onto her artist's sketch pad with her multi-coloured pencils while Mr Stone, the writer, photographed it with the camera that hung around his neck and seemed to be a part of him.

At dinner every night Mr Stone asked everyone what adventures they had and Nell asked him if he kept a log-book as she did. Mr Stone said he would like to see Nell's log-book and Rachel's sketch book so they could all compare notes. But Nell did not want her table companions to know what she had written about them in her log-book and Miss Leigh was just as reluctant to show anyone her sketch book because some of her drawings of some passengers showed them as she pictured them. She sketched Mrs Pearson, who was cuddly to look at, like a koala bear, and Mr Stone was portrayed as an old lion with a shaggy mane. She was kind to Grandma, who she sketched to look like a fairy godmother. Jan was sketched as an imp.

Nell had confided in Miss Leigh about her island Bodach and the artist had asked her to describe him in detail. So when Nell saw the sketch of the ship's Captain, she saw that Rachel had made him look just like the Bodach but not dripping sea water and without any seaweed in his hair.

Nell was glad Mr Stone and Mrs Pearson didn't see Miss Leigh's sketches and even more glad that the ship's Captain did not see the sketch of him, in case he made Miss Leigh walk the plank off the ship into the water, as the old pirate captains did to anyone who upset them.

So Miss Leigh did not show her sketches and paintings to anyone except Nell when they were in the library. And Nell let Miss Leigh read her log-book. Rachel was delighted at Nell's notes and - unlike Grandma - she did not lecture Nell about spelling. She also allowed Nell to look through her artist's bag, to look in her sketch books and helped her practise her drawing. Nell thought Rachel's drawings, sketches and paintings were more interesting than Mr Stone's photographs, which were colourful but not amusing.

Rachel started painting a picture of Grandma to give Grandma as a gift at the end of the voyage and Nell was fascinated to see how the artist produced a painting from rough sketches.

In only ten days after leaving England the passengers made many new friends and Nell's dinner table companions became close fellow travellers who exchanged their experiences and adventures.

Grandma!

Mrs Pearson

Mr Stone

Jan!

15th January
Yesterday Grandma and I went to the Captain's Party. Today it's getting hotter so I've been in my cabin drawing pictures of my new friends. Tonight we are going to listen to some music

and tom there is

CHAPTER THIRTEEN

Swimming with the Fish

*I*n the tenth day of the voyage, and four hours behind Greenwich Mean Time, the ship arrived at the British Virgin Islands and Nell and her two adopted aunts travelled from the ship by a small motor boat to the large island of Tortola, and on to the the magical little island of Virgin Gorda with its snow-white sandy beaches and turquoise waters and huge granite boulders on the shoreline.

Nell watched the many coloured butterflies, the brilliant plumed birds and the lush green plants - it was like a magical land, but the waters lapping the sparkling grey granite boulders were even more magical.

Dr Thompson brought along with her a goggle-box, which she held in the water to see the coral and fish. The local villagers also let Janet, Rachel and Nell borrow face goggles, snorkels and foot fins. Nell and Rachel quickly learnt the skill of snorkelling, which enabled them to swim and look below the surface at the fish and the sea bed. Nell had never before seen so many brightly coloured fish or sea shells, not even at the Sea Life Centre back in Scotland. Janet was taking photographs with her underwater camera while Rachel and Nell followed the instructions of the lifeguard who was also their swim leader. After that exciting expedition in the waters and along the beach Nell and her friends returned by the motor boat to the island of Tortola, where they had lunch of seafood and fruit and bought a T-shirt as a souvenir.

On returning to the ship, Nell met Jan in the children's recreation room and told him of her adventures on Tortola, the Treasure Island. Jan explained that he had been taken by his mother on an open-top safari bus through Tortola's town and villages, where he had heard Caribbean Calypso bands and visited souvenir shops and had bought a frightful native carnival mask.

That night, after their Tortola excursion, the
passengers went to sleep early because the
following day the liner would berth in another
magical Caribbean Island, Antigua.

A Goggle Box

CHAPTER FOURTEEN

A Magical Island

The next morning Nell and Grandma watched the ship tie up in the harbour of St Johns, the bustling capital of Antigua, with its colourful and noisy street traders and fragrant fruit markets. On the dockside a calypso band was playing stirring drum music to welcome them to the West Indies. The musicians were as colourful as their music and as cheerful as *Arcadia*, which was bedecked with bright bunting flags.

Grandma agreed that Nell could go with Janet and Rachel in a catamaran boat on a sail and snorkel excursion from one of Antigua's golden beaches. Jan was also on the catamaran called the Wadadli, which sailed out to a reef to see the shoals of multi-coloured fish and the bright white coral.

They stopped for lunch at 'Ma's Beach Restaurant', where they sat under straw-roofed huts and ate fresh tropical fruits, drank sweet milk from coconuts and chewed sugar cane which the local farmer cut for them on his nearby sugar plantation.

While listening to calypso music played on the beach by local villagers, Jan put on his gruesome carnival mask and ran up and down the beach, frightening the lady tourists until he stumbled in the sand and a lady took off his mask and put it on herself and chased Jan along the beach to everyone's merriment.

While Nell was enjoying the hot sun on the catamaran and beach, Grandma went shopping in the town and drank iced tea under palm trees in a bistro café near St John's Cathedral before she and Mrs Pearson together explored street markets for souvenirs.

When the passengers returned to the ship after their day in Antigua's tropical sun many of them looked like red lobsters that had been cooked on the beaches by the sun.

That night Grandma telephoned Grandpa from the cabin. When she phoned at 7.30 pm in the evening she awakened Grandpa because it was

11.30 pm, late at night in Scotland. Grandma had forgotten about the time zones and changing the clocks. While Nell was feeling sunburned and Grandma was talking about the tropical beaches and the 84°F temperature, Grandpa was shivering in the cold of Scotland and he told them that the snow was falling outside his window on the Island.

Outside the cabin window on *Arcadia,* the black frigate birds wheeled about over the harbour waters and the tall masts of a clipper windjammer ship called the *Mandalay.*

'Poor Grandpa in Scotland,' Nell thought as she wished him Goodnight or 'Oidhche mhath' in Gaelic. She counted the stars outside her cabin window and noticed that the new moon looked strangely upside down in the sky, unlike the moon back home. Very soon she was fast asleep.

CHAPTER FIFTEEN

Magic Moments

That night in her sleep Nell imagined she had seen the Bodach sitting on the rocks at Antigua's beautiful Blue Heron Bay. The Sea Spirit was disentangling a bundle of twisted nylon ropes that had entrapped a dolphin. Nearby another dolphin appeared, lying injured on the beach. It was cut by the propeller blade of a motor boat and was waiting for the Bodach.

At breakfast that morning Nell told Grandma what she had seen of the dolphins and the Bodach. Grandma smiled gently and told Nell that she must have been dreaming because she had only seen the Bodach in the Sea of the Hebrides. Later after breakfast Nell noticed the shoals of flying fish skimming over the waves and a school of dolphins surging and bobbing up and over the swell to keep up with the liner. They seemed to smile at Nell.

While Nell was standing at the ship's rails watching the dolphins, she told her marine biologist friend all about the Bodach and the injured dolphins. Janet listened carefully and explained to Nell the dangers of drifting nylon ropes and old fishing nets and oil spillage to marine and sea creatures.

'Just as land animals need vets,' she said, 'so sea creatures often need marine biologists to protect them. Whales, dolphins and seals can sometimes be hurt by the propellers of boats and ships.'

That evening after dinner Grandma and their table companions attended an entertainment in the ship's concert hall. The famous magician, Brett Sherwood, fascinated Nell, especially when he requested Grandma to lend him a five pound note. Grandma reluctantly opened her handbag and produced a Scottish five pound note, which puzzled the American magician who had never seen one before. He said it didn't look like a dollar or proper money and he immediately tore it in half and into small pieces of paper. Grandma was horrified and Nell was cross with the magician for tearing up Grandma's money. When Nell told him this he immediately produced the same whole Scottish five pound note from his pocket and gave it to Grandma, while he pulled a lollipop from behind Nell's ear. So they were friends again. But Grandma and Nell never volunteered again for any of the magician's tricks, although he often stopped and talked to Nell and Jan when he walked around the deck.

One day at the magician's show he asked for volunteers to be put inside a black box for a trick. No one stepped forward except Jan, who received applause from the audience and a lollipop from the magician. After that Jan said he also wanted to be a magician and he practised more tricks on everyone.

The next day Nell and Jan were walking on deck when Nell noticed a hawk perched on the ship's rigging near the funnel. Soon lots more passengers came to watch the bird. At night the hawk was still on the rigging and looked very weak. Mr Stone and Dr Thompson both agreed at dinner that the bird was perhaps migrating and had become lost or exhausted in recent storms and that it was roosting on the ship to rest. There was nothing anyone could do to help the hapless bird.

The next morning when Nell went on deck she saw Jan holding the hawk and feeding it with some meat. Jan explained that he had a pet hawk at home in Switzerland and he knew how to feed the bird. The ship's cook had given Jan some meat and a bowl of water and the bird rapidly recovered. Arrangements were made for Jan to feed the hawk

until it was strong enough to fly on again two days later. After that the crew and passengers regarded Jan with respect and thanks. Nell was proud he was her friend. Grandma bought him a special Knickerbocker Glory in the ice cream parlour and the crew gave Jan a ship's T-shirt and made him an honorary member of the crew. Even Madame Walrus smiled at him and hugged him till he managed to wriggle away from her.

The next day at the Sunday morning church service when the Captain conducted the service, Grandma played the piano and Mrs Pearson read the lesson. Jan didn't look very comfortable during the service because he was not accustomed to the sea like Nell and he began to look sea-sick again, so he left the service to go into the fresh air. Nell found him leaning over the ship's rail and soon the nurse came and gave him some tablets and water. The nurse thanked Nell for helping Jan, who was too embarrassed to say anything.

CHAPTER SIXTEEN

Fancy Dress Party

Jan had recovered by the next evening for the Carnival Night celebration when everybody appeared in fancy dress. Nell dressed up as a mermaid and found it difficult to walk in a fish's tail! Grandma dressed as Florence Nightingale and Mr Stone wore a false beard as the Bodach, Spirit of the Sea. Dr Thompson dressed as the Queen of the Sea and Miss Leigh was a colourful Lady Britannia. Mrs Pearson dressed as a Victorian lady. Jan appeared with his father dressed as the Swiss hero William Tell, and the boy with an apple on his head.

Then all the ship's cooks, waitresses and stewards entered the Dining Room in a long Conga line, singing and dancing around the room, and some of the passengers, including Nell and Jan, joined in the fun and the long dancing line.

The next night Grandma allowed Nell to stay up late to hear a lecture on the top deck about Astronomy and the night sky, given by a lady ship's officer. She explained the position of the stars in the clear night sky, the constellations and how in ancient times sailors steered by the stars. Nell asked her why the moon looked upside down in the Southern Seas and the lady astronomer said she would explain it in the next lecture, when she was sure she would have the right answer.

Sixteen days after leaving England the *Arcadia* arrived at the Panama Canal which joins the Caribbean Sea to the Pacific Ocean. Nell went with her table companions on a small motor boat to visit the little islands of San Blas, where the natives were small people not much bigger than Nell and whose hair and eyes were as black as coal but their necklaces were as multi-coloured as rainbows. The small children gathered in a noisy crowd around Mr Stone, chanting 'Santa Claus! Santa Claus!' and pointing to his long white hair and bushy white moustache. Although it was some time after Christmas, the village children seemed to think that Father Christmas had returned to their island. But the village headman explained that Mr Stone was from the big ship and was not Santa Claus.

It was the poverty, the lack of fresh water and food on the San Blas islands that surprised Nell, who gave her Scottish coins to an old grandmother who was surrounded by a dozen hungry, crying infants. Nell and Jan went with some of the older children into the straw huts built on stilts over the water and saw where the families all lived together in what were like wooden garden sheds with straw roofs and plank floors but without any heating and lighting.

That night at dinner Nell was quiet while she remembered the thin, gaunt faces of the hungry island children whose only pleasure seemed to be swimming in the warm Caribbean waters, or stringing beads on necklaces outside the straw-roofed huts in the 90-degree burning sun.

After the ship slowly made passage through the Panama Canal, the *Arcadia* headed for Honolulu, one of the Hawaiian Islands, then Fiji, New Caledonia and on to Australia. As they made passage through Guatemala Bay, Nell and Grandma saw turtles

swimming outside the cabin window.

They also saw a replica of Captain Cook's ship, the Endeavour, which took the explorer to Australia from England and was now re-enacting the historic voyage. The replica ship looked so small in the ocean with its three sails and its brown and white hull tossing up and down in the heavy sea swell. Nell admired the courage of Captain Cook and his small crew in their small sailing ship to sail from England for months on stormy seas to ever reach Australia.

CHAPTER SEVENTEEN

Pineapples Galore

When the *Arcadia* eventually reached the American Pacific Ocean State of Hawaii, called the Aloha State, the ship docked at Honolulu where they were greeted on the dockside by a Hawaiian hula band and a choir of beautiful ladies in grass skirts and necklaces of orchid flowers called leis.

The passengers were immediately taken on a coach tour of Honolulu past the Queen Emma Royal Palace where they had no time to stop for afternoon tea. Nell with Grandma, Janet, Rachel and Jan were all driven to the waterside for an excursion on a yellow submarine, a voyage which took the party down to a depth of 100 feet to see shoals of colourful fish swimming among the reefs.

After that their coach took them on an island tour to Waikiki Beach, which is a paradise for swimmers and surfers, then on to the rainforest, the Botanical Gardens with marvellous orchids and exotic blooms, and then to a pineapple plantation. Here there were thousands of plants bearing pineapples that were harvested by women wearing thick gloves to protect them from the spiky leaves. Then the fruit would be canned and sent in tins to countries all over the world, including Scotland, where Nell ate pineapple chunks with ice cream. At the plantation shop Nell was shown many different ways to cut and serve the sweet yellow pineapples.

Nell and Grandma collected various recipes for pineapple meals and desserts but the party had to return to the ship before it cast off its mooring to continue southwards across the Equator on the the South Pacific Islands of Fiji, where *Arcadia's* passengers could again explore more Pacific Islands.

Soon the ship was approaching the Equator, which is an imaginary line that encircles the world and divides the globe into the northern and southern hemispheres, like a string around the middle of an orange. The Equator is

not visible on the sea, but it is clearly marked
on all the atlases and charts and it is a very real
marker for navigation to mariners who need
 to use their charts, because there are no
signposts on the sea.

CHAPTER EIGHTEEN

Crossing the Equator

As the ship neared the Equator, the ship's Purser, who manages the ship for the Captain, announced that the Captain had an important message for all the passengers and crew. Everyone was quiet and only the cries of the seagulls could be heard when the Captain explained that King Neptune, the Ruler of the Sea, had come aboard the ship with his Queen Amphitrite and his courtiers to conduct the traditional ceremony of 'Crossing the line', which has been celebrated by seafarers of all nations when they cross the Equator for the first time. The purpose of the ritual is to pacify the spirits of the Equator where storms blow up to sink ships and where hurricanes and typhoons are spawned.

The Captain ordered all members of the crew who had not crossed the Equator before to submit themselves to King Neptune for the initiation ceremony. This is a mock baptism of novices who are ducked in the King's big tub of green slimy smelly water, which he says will cleanse them of all the dirt of the cities of the north.

When Jan heard this he became quite pale because he had been made an honorary crew member and now he would be ducked with the ship's chefs, cabin boys and engineers in the green tub.

The Captain then introduced King Neptune, who had a straggly beard and a golden crown, and was sitting on a barnacle-covered throne on a platform. He was holding a long trident spear to prod the Court Jester and anyone who didn't do what they were told.

On one side of the King was his green tub with fearsome guards with big swords and his courtiers, who included a fierce-looking barber with big scissors for cutting off people's hair as well as mischievous knaves and men dressed as bears who ducked the novices in the big tub.

On the other side of King Neptune sat Queen Amphitrite, who looked like an old witch and cackled like an old hen when the King prodded the Jester towards the bears, who ducked him in the

tub. Jan hid behind Madame Walrus and tried to take off his crew T-shirt, but she pinched his ear and made him stand out.

The old sea-witch Queen spotted Jan and pointed to him and the pastry chef, who was wearing his tall white hat. Nell felt sorry for Jan and her favourite chef when the bears grabbed them and took them to King Neptune. The King then led a parade around the ship before he returned to his throne beside the swimming pool. He then ordered his courtiers to duck Jan in the green water tub.

But the ship's Master raised his hand and told King Neptune that Jan had saved the hawk. So the King ordered Jan to be released and for the Jester to be put in the tub in his place. This made the old Queen cackle again and this time she opened her mouth so wide that her false teeth fell into the swimming pool.

Nell immediately jumped into the pool and managed to retrieve the false teeth. Everyone cheered Nell, who gave Jan the dentures to return to the toothless Queen, who then presented Nell and Jan each with a big conch shell.

King Neptune asked them their names and where they came from. He told Jan he had never been to Switzerland because that land of mountains is in the middle of Europe and so far away from the sea.

When Nell explained that she was from Scotland and her name was Nell, the King looked very pleased and said in his deep, resonant voice, which sounded like a rumbling waterfall, 'Well, well, well. I don't meet many children from snowy Switzerland nor mountainous Scotland here on the Equator. I wonder if you know my good friend Bodach Na Mara, the Spirit of the Sea?'

Nell told him that the Bodach often visited her Island in the Hebrides. 'And he gave me the name Leanabh na goith, Child of the Wind. I saw the Bodach recently in the Blue Heron Bay in the Caribbean, helping injured dolphins,' she said. 'The Bodach says in Gaelic "Nach Uramach an Cuan", which means "How worthy of honour is the Sea," and I do honour the sea and sea life.'

King Neptune and even his old Queen, the fierce courtiers and the Jester all looked very pleased and applauded Nell. King Neptune bellowed, 'May the spirits of the sea protect you, Nell.'

Then the King stood up and, waving his trident spear, ordered his guards and the bears to

escort Nell and Jan with the chef to the throne. When the brave trio stood before him the King presented them each with a beautiful official certificate signed and sealed by his maritime majesty and solemnly witnessed by the ship's Master, which testified that the trio had officially 'crossed the line' and they were excused from the green tub ducking any time they crossed the Equator again.

After everyone had admired King Neptune's certificates and the royal court had left the ship,

Grandma said she would rather fly in an aeroplane across the Equator than be ducked in the green tub.

The pastry chef led Nell, Jan and Grandma and their friends to the ice cream parlour to cool off with treats of milkshakes. The chef also invited Grandma and Madame Walrus to visit the ship's galley, which is the giant kitchen where all the food is prepared by a team of chefs.

A couple of days later, after the ship had crossed from the northern hemisphere to the southern hemisphere, the ship crossed the International Date Line. Because the ship's clocks were put back again it became the Day that Never Was. No one ever explained to Nell how a day could be lost. Grandma said she would ask the Captain to find the lost day or give her a refund of her fare for the Day that Never Was.

Various passengers had told Nell that when the ship crossed from the northern to southern hemisphere, the water in the cabin washbasin would fall down the drain anticlockwise instead of clockwise but she never saw that due to the pitching and rolling of the ship. Or perhaps it was not true.

As the liner continued on its voyage, King Neptune and his court slowly disappeared beneath the deep Equatorial waters. Arcadia had just one more stop before Australia, and that was the South Sea islands of Fiji. Nell and Jan decided that because they knew nothing about Fiji they would both go to the ship's library to read and learn about the islands. There they met Mr Stone, who was studying a geography book with Mrs Pearson and Grandma. He told the children that the Fiji Islands are called the Enchanted Isles and the Land of Smiles, with white sand beaches and crystal blue seas with lots of green turtles and exotic birds and coconut palms.

'There are also tropical fruits, orchids and ginger and sugar plantations as well as temples and even golden mosques and gold mines,' he told them. 'The Fijian people are very friendly, but instead of greeting people with "Hello" they say "Bula Bula". Fiji is a land of extinct volcanoes and the Fijians have a strange national sport of fire-walking. Look out too for their national drink - instead of tea or coffee they drink a fiery brew of peppers called Kava, which tastes like cough mixture.'

CHAPTER NINETEEN

On the Island of Cannibals

Jan wanted to know if there are still any cannibals on the Fijian islands, but Mr Stone shook his head and said, 'Certainly not.' But he warned the children not to drop litter on the paradise islands because, although the islanders were friendly, they did not like litterbugs. He also explained that anyone who took away any living marine creature would be dealt with by the frizzy-haired natives as a thief.

Mr Stone advised them, 'Take only photographs from the island and leave nothing but your footprints on the clean beaches for the tide to wash away.'

So when the great ship eventually cruised into the loveliest of the Fijian Islands, called Yasawa-I-Rara, Nell and Jan with Rachel and Janet hurried onto one of the ship's launches to take them to the palm-fringed little island paradise where the white sand was like warm icing sugar and the towering coconut trees above them whispered gentle sounds in the soothing breeze.

While Janet and Rachel sat down on a rug to prepare a picnic, Nell and Jan ran along the beach to the biggest coconut tree, which had coconuts the size of footballs hanging on it. They were both looking up and counting the huge coconuts when a deep voice behind the tree growled, 'Bula Bula'. There then appeared a giant brown man with frizzy black hair, a smile with large white teeth, a yellow flower in his ear and a shark's tooth necklace. He looked like one of those famous Fiji rugby players but he was even more fearsome with his big coconut cutting knife in one hand and a monster coconut in the other.

Nell was so terrified that all she could do was remember to mumble 'Bula Bula' in reply. But Jan was so scared he was speechless until Nell whispered to him to say 'Bula Bula' as well.

Then the Fiji giant smiled at them and lifted up his great knife and with one blow and a loud roar of his voice he sliced off the top of the coconut and offered it to Jan and Nell to drink the sweet, warm coco milk.

Then they all walked back to Janet and Rachel, who offered the Fiji giant some afternoon picnic sandwiches and teacakes. He could speak very good English and he told them all about his island. When they finished their picnic they all went with the Bula Bula man exploring the beach and places called the Pirates Den and Fish Patch and they all swam and splashed each other in the warm seawater.

They were all laughing and dancing along the beach when a European teenager walked past them and dropped a cigarette packet on the white sand. The Fiji man chased the litterbug, shook his shark's tooth at him and made him walk back to pick up his litter. When the young man did that the Fiji giant smiled again and

wished them all a safe voyage to Australia and told them, 'Leave only your footprints in the sand, not your litter.'

They then returned to the ship on the launch boats. Nell and Jan told Mr Stone about their Fiji adventure and the litterbug teenager who got chased by the angry Bula giant.

Then heavy black clouds darkened the skies and the weather soon worsened. There was monsoon rain and mist as the ship left Fiji with the natives waving goodbye and shouting 'Bon Voyage'.

CHAPTER TWENTY

The Terrible Storm

Shortly afterwards, a cyclone which the weatherman called Ella blew up in the area of Tonga. At the same time another cyclone called Rona was hurtling towards Queensland in Australia where Nell's parents lived. Neither Nell nor anyone else on the ship could understand why the weather experts gave such nice girls' names to such nasty cyclones, which blow down forests and houses and sink ships at sea and are worse than the gales in Europe.

As the weather worsened, the Captain gathered with his navigator and ship's officer on the bridge to discuss the dangers. The Captain ordered the helmsman to alter the ship's course and to cruise full steam ahead directly to Australia and the safety of the harbour in the city of Sydney and to avoid the terrible cyclones.

But the storm did break and torrential rain deluged the ship and all the deck chairs had to be taken inside for safety. The passengers hurried to their snug warm cabins to watch the rain and storm from their porthole windows or gather in the recreation rooms or library to discuss how the ship would get to Australia through rough seas with a sea-swell as high as a lorry. Passengers also listened to the ship's radio announcements and the Captain's messages of reassurance and informing them of their progress.

Grandma and Mr Stone played Scrabble while Rachel sketched the passengers, and Janet told Nell and Jan about marine biology and Mrs Pearson told stories about Australia.

When the weather improved, many passengers rushed out on to the sun decks again for sunbathing or swimming in the pool. After 42 days of the voyage, *Arcadia* approached the coast of Australia in very hot weather and bright sunshine of 85°F. Jan was the first to sight land with his telescope, so he won another T-shirt.

CHAPTER TWENTY ONE

Land Ho! Australia at Last!

The liner made her passage through the north and south headlands into Sydney Harbour under Sydney Harbour Bridge, which looks like a metal coat-hanger, into Darling Harbour.

They had travelled 14,651 miles from England. They had arrived in Australia after journeying around the world and had arrived safely. So the passengers all held hands in a great circle and sang 'Auld Lang Syne' and exchanged their names and addresses and promised to write to each other. Jan gave Nell his beloved telescope and she gave him her Island lucky charm called a luckenbooth to keep him safe in Australia where his father was going to work as an aeroplane pilot.

There was a brass band in the harbour playing welcoming music and hundreds of friends and relatives were waiting to greet the ship's passengers.

When the great liner was moored to the dockside everyone cheered the Captain and his crew to thank them for safely bringing them around the world through high seas and storms to down under.

As the passengers disembarked to join their families, there was happy shouting and clapping and lots of coloured streamers, balloons and flags.

Grandma held up her umbrella with a tartan ribbon tied on it so that Nell's parents could see Grandma in the crowd.

'Welcome to Australia!' shouted Nell's father, Jack, when he spotted them. Nell's mother, May, was so happy she was crying with tears of joy. There were lots of hugs and kisses and then the whole family tumbled into a big taxi to go to a big hotel to recover from the voyage before the long journey to Queensland.

Grandma said she felt funny because she had been at sea for so long it felt that the land and the taxi were wobbling like the ship, which made the driver laugh. 'I shall have to find my land-legs before I can walk far,' she said.

They were still all laughing with happiness at their reunion. Mother had stopped weeping for joy and Grandma soon said that the Australian ground wasn't wobbling any more. When they reached the hotel for their first day in Australia, and before Nell closed her eyes to sleep, the Child of the Wind closed her log-book of the voyage and opened her new Australian adventure book to start tomorrow her next story, which she would call *Nell in Australia*.

Nell in Australia

- Book Three -

Now that Nell and Grandma have travelled halfway around the world and arrived in Australia, Nell awakens to a new country with exciting new people and astonishing new animals. In this new land Nell of the Seas makes new friends and has new adventures in fascinating regions.

CHAPTER ONE

In Port at Last – The Family Reunion

On their arrival in Australia after their epic worldwide voyage of 40 days and 40 nights in the wilderness of the high seas, Nell and Grandma were both glad to step ashore on dry land. They were delighted to be reunited with Mother and Father again, but sorry that Grandpa couldn't be with them yet. He was back in Scotland keeping the island ferry going to the mainland.

In the icy cold Atlantic the seals and seabirds are struggling against the swirling ocean currents and tides. The fishing boats and ferry are moored for safety in the lee of the hills in the little harbour. Grandpa is waiting for the gales to abate and the tide to turn. The old seaman has seen it all before in his sixty years on the islands in all the times before his hair grew as white as the sea foam.

On the other side of the world in Australia at the same time in February the sun is hot and the sea is calm and warm. Not only are the seasons of the year different, so that at Christmas it is like a hotter summer with no snow, the time by the clocks is different, so that Australian clocks are 12 hours behind the old Wag at the Wall clock in Nell's home.

Grandpa once tried to explain it all to Nell. He said that the sun and the earth were like two spheres in the heaven and each day the earth circled the sun.

'Our earth is just like a cog in the wheel of the time machine of the universe, Nell,' he had said.

And while Grandpa was sitting in the winter darkness by the smoky peat fire he was studying a world atlas by the old lamp to follow the voyage of Nell and Grandma.

At the same time, Nell and Grandma were awakening. When Nell jumped out of bed and looked through the large open window the very bright Aussie summer sun cast a golden glow over the lovely city of Sydney with its blue waters of beautiful Darling Harbour and nearby Botany Bay.

This was the same Botany Bay where, 200 years ago, convict prisoners were transported by sailing ship from Scotland for poaching a salmon or stealing a sheep. These wretched prisoners included women convicted for stealing a loaf of bread, and were sent to Australia to colonize the continent. The prisoners were called Prisoners of His Majesty (POMS) and today their great, great, great grandchildren still live and work in Australia as doctors, lawyers, scientists and farmers.

Nell was trying to imagine how the prisoners survived their many months' long passage in crowded sailing ships as she gazed out at Sydney's famous Opera House, which glistens like white sails. And across the waters is the famous Anzac Bridge which spans the harbour.

81

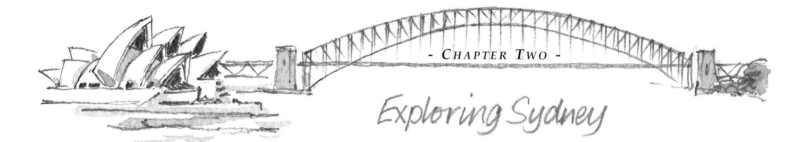

CHAPTER TWO

Exploring Sydney

After a good night's sleep, breakfast was needed before they began their great trek into the Australian continent to Mother and Father's new home, which was a wooden bungalow in Queensland near the Great Barrier Reef, where Father works to protect the marine creatures and the coral. Father took Mother, Nell and Grandma in an elevator up the city's skyscraper Centre Point Tower Restaurant which stands like a sentinel over Sydney. This is Australia's oldest city, where 2 million people live, and with a huge Olympic Park built for the Millennium 2000 Olympic Games.

The morning sun was already so hot that instead of their daily breakfast porridge, the Anderson family selected fruit juices and plates of fresh fruit, macadamia nuts and warm bread and golden honey from the buffet table that was as long as a shop counter.

The skyscraper was so high up in the cloudless blue sky that in the gentle breeze the tower swayed sideways an inch. Grandma looked alarmed and said it was like being in an aeroplane and she wanted to whizz down in the elevator to the firm ground in the streets of the shopping centre below.

Father gave Nell and Grandma some shiny Australian dollar coins to buy themselves wide-brimmed straw hats and sun block to protect them in the bright sun. He then explained that he was taking them in a car to visit a real working outback colonial farm called Gledswood.

Grandma waved her hat with joy to be going into the countryside after six weeks sailing the wide oceans and mountainous seas in the pitching and rolling ship. She was looking forward to having tea served in a china pot and newly baked scones with strawberry jam and fresh farm cream. Mother explained that the outback homesteads did not have Scottish scones but they did have dampers, that are like bread and water pancakes. It would be a special picnic in the country.

CHAPTER THREE

A Ride in 'Old Jalopy'

So the whole Anderson family squeezed into an ancient open-topped truck which Father called 'Old Jalopy' and off they drove out of Sydney, past the Olympic stadium on the dusty roads into the bushland to the old historical homestead of Gledswood.

Old Jalopy wasn't very fast. 'Thank goodness,' said Grandma, but they all held onto their sun hats as they watched the strange animals and rainbow-coloured birds in the outback grassland that smelled of sweet flowers and herbs. They passed old farmhouses selling honey, fruit, nuts and vegetables. Grandma kept wanting to stop to talk to the farmers' wives. Father said they would not get to Gledswood if they kept stopping.

Before they got to the homestead the sun was so hot that Old Jalopy's engine started steaming like a tea kettle on the peat fire in their Scottish Island cottage back home, so they put their drinking water in the motor to cool it down in the 80°F temperature.

When they arrived at the colonial farm with its multi-coloured garden and rolling lush pastures, the Anderson family were greeted by the friendly Australian farm folk. Their warm-hearted hospitality made Nell and Grandma feel at home as they sat in the garden seats. Grandma was delighted when she was served with tea in a china teapot on a silver tray and Nell was given iced juices and ice sorbets, while Father and Mother had glasses of cold Australian wine and gourmet quiches. When the family were recovered from their journey they exchanged stories with the Gledswood family. Then the Andersons were taken on a tour around the farm on a horse-drawn buggy, which was like a step back into history.

Nell and Grandma were aghast to learn that the lovely old-fashioned stone farmhouse had been built by convicts two centuries earlier.

Chapter Four

Boomerang Games

Then, while they were sitting on a wooden bench beneath a great eucalyptus tree admiring the rolling pastures, the farm's suntanned shepherd, Ben, whistled to his sleek black sheepdog Jet. The shepherd then pointed to a big woolly merino ram and signalled the dog to steer the horned sheep into the shearing shed. Then the shepherd sheared the ram of all its valuable woollen fleece quicker than Nell could comb her hair. Ben offered some of the wool to Grandma to take home for spinning and knitting a pair of socks for Grandpa.

Ben then took them outside the shearing shed to the pasture. There he demonstrated the art of boomerang throwing. Nell had never seen a boomerang before. It looked like a flat curved stick as long as her arm. When the shepherd threw it far away in the air the boomerang turned and whizzed back to him like a whirring bird, which he caught with his outstretched hand. Jet wagged his tail and chased the stick and raced back to his master all breathless and with his tongue hanging out. He then sat at the shepherd's feet and wagged his tail and rolled on his back. Ben stroked the dog and passed the boomerang for Nell to throw.

Grandma was sitting nearby drinking tea under the shade of her wide sun hat with the farmer's wife. Grandma told Nell to be careful not to let the stick boomerang back to hit the teapot.

When Ben showed Nell the special way to hold the flat side of the boomerang and how to throw it she jumped up and down excitedly with delight as if she was doing the Highland Fling. But when Nell threw it, the stick just fell to the ground nearby. Jet ambled over to it in the grass and retrieved it for Nell. The dog looked disdainfully at Nell, shook his shaggy head and sat beside her.

Nell had time to try again because her father was exploring the wine cellar and her mother was in the farm kitchen talking to the cook about

Gledswood salads. When he saw Nell practising, the farmer was so pleased that he gave her a boomerang to take home to her schoolfriends in Scotland.

CHAPTER FIVE

Waltzing Matilda

By the time it was ready to go, Old Jalopy had cooled down after the farmer had put cold water from the well in the engine. So the Anderson family all waved goodbye and shouted the farewells to the friendly Gledswood folk and Jet, who chased the car down the dusty road, and barked at Nell, who was in the back seat holding her sun hat and waving the boomerang.

As they motored over the dusty roads Father taught all the family how to sing Australia's famous national song 'Waltzing Matilda' about a jolly swagman sitting by a billabong under a tree brewing tea. This made Grandma laugh.

By the time they reached Sydney all the Andersons were singing the song together like a real choir and the people they passed in the settlements and towns all waved and smiled at them, especially when Grandma waved the sun hat at them as if she was the Queen.

Once a jolly swagman camped by a billabong under the shade of a Coolabah tree... and he sang as he watched and waited while his billy boiled "Who'll come a-waltzing Matilda with me?"

CHAPTER SIX

Adventures in the Outback

The next day Father took the family in Old Jalopy westwards out of Sydney into the Australian Bush to the Wildlife Zoo Park.

The cuddly koalas in the trees looked so sleepy that Grandma worried they might fall off. They hardly moved when Nell fed them their favourite meal of eucalyptus leaves. But the red-necked wallabies were wide awake. They hopped about between the emus and the fairy penguins.

Grandma wanted to feed the kangaroos. But when she told the zookeeper that the roos were smelly and needed a good wash, especially behind the ears, the roos pricked up their ears and bounded away in great leaps.

'They must have heard you, Grandma!' said Nell.

'The only creatures here who like the water are the crocodiles,' said the zookeeper.

Grandma shivered with fright. 'You won't catch me going anywhere near crocodiles,' she said firmly.

Nell said she would throw a banana to the big croc in the pond. The crocodile was like a long log. He suddenly opened his eyes and snapped his great jaws full of long sharp teeth. Nell dropped the banana with fright and ran away.

The kookaburra birds and gaudy parrots were laughing noisily in the gum trees.

Grandma was happy to leave the boisterous birds and animals of the zoo and travel to the Paramatta River and visit the 'Big Bush' countryside. So the Anderson family followed in the footsteps of the first explorers, the overlanders and swagmen, along the trail to the rugged Blue Mountains at Katoomba.

CHAPTER SEVEN

The Blue Mountains

Whoever heard of blue mountains!' said Nell, who had only ever seen the snow-capped Scottish mountains of Ben Nevis and Ben More above the Scottish glens.

But at Katoomba the mountains really do look blue. Father explained that it is because of the blue haze caused by the fragrant eucalyptus oil evaporating from the gum trees.

'I doubt it,' said Grandma. 'I think it really comes from the blue smoke of the Aboriginal tribesmen's campfires.'

Father disagreed and this led to a dispute between Grandma and Father which was only settled by Mother saying that it could be both reasons.

The family lunched at a mountain lodge deep in the bush. Then they returned to Sydney to visit the city's huge Olympic Games Park. It is so big it could seat 100,000 spectators from all over the world to see sportsmen and women from all nations compete for gold medals.

After their day's hectic adventures and sightseeing, the Andersons returned to their skyscraper hotel. Nell just wanted to sit by the window and look out at the city's lights and the bay. But she had promised Grandpa back in Scotland that she would keep her diary for him, so she began writing about her adventures. Her eyes filled with tears when she thought of poor old Grandpa back in frosty Scotland eating his porridge by he kitchen stove waiting for the postman to bring letters to him and looking out of the window at the cold Atlantic Ocean, the home of the Old Man of the Seas. So Nell decided she would write him a long letter and immediately started 'Dear Grandpa.'

An hour later when she finished writing she tumbled into bed. She was soon dreaming of Blue Mountains, red-necked wallabies, smelly roos, rainbow parrots and homestead savoury quiche and honeyed fruits.

She also dreamed of her big day tomorrow -

it would be her first aeroplane flight. Nell and her family were to fly to the small outback town of Alice Springs and the famous Ayers Rock. This is the world's largest rock and is in the Australian outback.

CHAPTER EIGHT

To Alice Springs and Ayers Rock

Grandma was prepared to overcome her reluctance to fly to Alice Springs because she wanted to meet her cousin Jemimah, whom she had not met since childhood. Jemimah had emigrated as a schoolgirl with her family from Scotland over half a century ago.

At Sydney Airport Nell excitedly watched the arrival and departure of all sorts and sizes of aeroplanes and helicopters that roared in and out along the tarmac.

Grandma covered her ears and again complained that only birds are meant to fly. She repeated that she didn't like heights. But Nell reminded Grandma that she was happy to travel in Grandpa's fishing boat and the island ferry at their home on the Island of Seil and to travel in an ocean liner over the Seven Seas. Nell's parents also agreed with what she had learned at school, that travel by aeroplane is as safe as by a ship or car.

Grandma did not look convinced; she said she would like a cup of tea while she waited to board the big silver plane.

Nell preferred to explore the airport shops with her mother. She was scanning the bookshelves when someone shouted her name. When she glanced up she saw the Swiss boy Jan Hesterberg, who had been on the ship with them. He was waving to her across the shop aisle. His mother, Frau Hesterberg, was with him and they explained that they were also going to Alice Springs where they were to meet his father, who was a pilot delivering post to the outback homesteads.

Frau Hesterberg was pleased to meet the Anderson family again. They exchanged their impressions of Australia. Jan's mother said she missed the snow-capped Alps and felt lost in the vastness of the boundless outback.

Soon they were all boarding the aeroplane. Nell sat in a window seat with Jan beside her. Grandma did not want to look out of the window

and the adults all chatted together.

As the engines roared, the plane rose from the tarmac and soared skywards. Grandma tightened her safety belt even more and shut her eyes.

Nell was so thrilled that she would have jumped up with excitement but she was held safely in her seat by the safety belt. As the plane soared higher above the clouds, Jan explained to Nell how aeroplanes can fly, even though they are heavier than air. He also showed her his Swiss pocket compass and explained the basic points of the compass and navigation.

As the aeroplane continued its ascent everything on the ground thousands of feet below grew smaller and smaller. And as they flew further inland to central Australia, the land below grew redder and redder with little grey/green blobs of what were spinifax trees.

High Above the Clouds

The smartly uniformed Qantas stewardess spoke different languages to the different passengers and brought trays of drinks and meals round. She enjoyed speaking foreign languages. When Nell greeted her in Gaelic with 'Latha math dhut fhein. Ciamar a tha thu?' the stewardess laughed with delight. She replied in a little Gaelic that her mother had emigrated from Scotland and had taught her a little of the 'auld language' of the Highlands. She also chatted to Grandma in Gaelic about the 'auld country' and invited Grandma to look out of the cabin window at the white clouds.

Grandma said she wanted to know how the pilot knew where he was driving when he was flying through the clouds.

The stewardess had to serve the other passengers so Jan showed Grandma his compass and he and Nell explained that the pilot's navigation was just the same as Grandpa's navigation of his ferry through the Scotch mist around the Western Isles of Scotland. That comforted Grandma.

The stewardess complimented the Swiss boy on his good English and Nell for speaking Gaelic and she presented both of them with an airline T-shirt.

A few hours later the plane landed in Alice Springs, the small town in the outback. When Nell stepped out of the air-conditioned plane it was so hot that it felt like the inside of Grandma's kitchen oven. The sunshine was also so bright that Nell was glad that Grandma had told her to bring her sun hat and sunblock.

At the airport Great Aunt Jemimah was waiting to greet the Anderson family. She was a little old lady who had white hair that was even whiter than Grandma's hair. Although she seemed a lot older than Grandma, there was a family resemblance and they both had hair tied up at the back of their heads in what is called a Victoria bun.

There were hugs and kisses and laughter by all the Andersons, which seemed to make all the passengers happy.

After collecting their luggage from the baggage carousel in the cool airport lounge, the passengers boarded the hotel courtesy coach to take them to their hotel in Alice Springs. On the way, the coach driver stopped the bus to allow three camels to amble across the road. Grandma was bothered and asked, 'Are we in Australia or Africa? I didn't know there were camels in Australia!'

The coach driver and Great Aunt Jemimah assured Grandma there really are camels on the southern continent to trek across the hot, arid outback. Aunt Jemimah said she could arrange for Grandma to have a ride on a camel but Grandma said she would rather let Nell and Jan, who she called 'the Swiss laddie', have the experience instead of her.

Australia's Unusual Radio School

After they had left their luggage at the hotel, Great Aunt Jemimah had a surprise for the two children. She proudly took them to Australia's unique School of the Air.

She beamed with pride as she explained it was the biggest classroom in the world. Instead of blackboards and school desks, this school came to the pupils' own homes by radio.

Both Nell and Jan said their schools in Scotland and Switzerland were nothing like the radio school. They both said they would like to have lessons broadcast by two-way radio to them in their own homes. That would be better than having to wake up early in the cold winter mornings to travel to school in the rain or snow.

'But if I stayed at home for all my lessons I would miss all my friends, and my teacher, Miss Murray. She's really good at Gaelic,' said Nell.

'I wouldn't miss my teacher,' said Jan. 'He's called Herr Muff and he's gruff and grumpy and gives us lots of homework in French, German and Italian and he expects us to learn English. But I suppose I would miss going skiing, horse riding and mountaineering with my friends,' he added.

Grandma and Great Aunt Jemimah then exchanged recollections and tales of their childhood over half a century earlier. In those far off days as schoolgirls they sat in rows of bench seats in cold classrooms with a smoking peat fire which produced more smoke than heat. Then they had to wear woollen mittens to keep their hands warm when they wrote with scratchy pens in exercise books. They had to stand up in class and each recite their arithmetic tables aloud in English and Gaelic.

The Flying Doctors

The two white-haired old ladies were so busy telling the children how lucky they are now instead of fifty years ago that Nell and Jan were glad when Mother and Father took them off to see an exhibition about Australia's Royal Flying Doctor Service, the RFDS. Each year their planes fly the equivalent of 650 times around the world, treating more than 150,000 patients and making nearly 125,000 evacuation flights. It illustrated how doctors fly aeroplanes to outback farms to treat anyone who is ill or injured. At home on her Scottish Island, Nell's lady doctor travels about the Island in an old car and by ferry. In an emergency the helicopter or lifeboat takes the patients to the mainland hospital.

Jan explained that in Switzerland, post or mail buses transported both the mail and the passengers around the Alpine villages. There is also a similar flying doctor service by helicopter.

Great Aunt Jemimah told them how Alice Springs was named after a girl, and showed them the quiet pool of water in the middle of the dusty riverbed. It is not a spring like the springs in Scotland and Switzerland, but it is a fault in the water-table, through which water seeps. Nell felt she was back at school having a Geography lesson. But she liked watching the pink birds sitting in the trees and flying around looking rather like small pink parrots. Grandma was fascinated to see the historic old telegraph station. The rooms still had the original furniture from years ago.

CHAPTER TWELVE

Nell's New Friends

Nell and Jan were thrilled to see two orphaned baby kangaroos. The warden explained how they had to be looked after as if they were in their mother's pouch until they were older. Baby kangaroos are called 'Joeys' in Australia.

Another surprise by Aunt Jemimah followed. She took them all on a walkabout town tour of Alice Springs. First stop was the Todd River, which was not a river at all, but a dusty sandbed with not a drop of water.

Nell and Jan waved to some Aboriginal children who were lounging in the shade of a gum tree by the Todd River bridge. The tribal children had their own language just as Nell spoke Gaelic and Jan spoke French and German. However, they could all talk together by speaking English. The children all laughed when they spoke their own languages as well as English. The Aboriginal boy, who was a 'ten-ager' like Jan, said he wanted to go to university in Melbourne to study to be a lawyer. His sister, who was eight years old like Nell, said she also wanted to go to university with her brother but she wanted to be a doctor to care for her own people on the settlement. Nell said she would send them a postcard when she one day

Joey in Blanket Pouch

returned to Scotland and Jan promised to send one from Switzerland, but it might not be for a long time.

After they said their farewells, Grandma said she would like to visit the local opal gemstone museum to see the beautiful Australian rainbow crystal opals that Great Aunt Jemimah had said changed colour like a kaleidoscope when you moved them. Unfortunately Grandma could not afford to buy an opal.

So on they went to the Aboriginal Dreamtime Art Gallery to see the folk art, the pottery and the carvings. Grandma could afford to buy a beautifully painted flower vase, which she gave to Father and Mother for their new home in Queensland.

All that was enough for one day. So they all returned to the hotel for a swim in the swimming pool before dinner and a good night's sleep because they had to awake early next morning for another big surprise.

Chapter Thirteen

Flying a Balloon

So at dawn Nell and Jan went off for another exhilarating adventure - a hot-air balloon flight. It was necessary to start early in the quiet of the morning when the air is fresh and the wind is only gentle.

The balloon was huge, with multi-coloured stripes and a large wicker basket the size of a car below it, with a gas burner to heat the air for the balloon to ascend skywards. It rose gently and quietly - much more smoothly, quietly and more stately than a noisy aeroplane. Soon they glided over the scenic MacDonnell mountain ranges and saw lots of animals below them. After an hour in the sky the pilot gently lowered the giant balloon and when the big basket touched the ground they all jumped out. Then they were treated to a balloonist outdoor breakfast of chicken, bread, honey and for the first time ever for Nell and Jan a sip of champagne to celebrate their magical flight. They were also presented with a flight certificate. After that Jan said he wasn't sure now

if he wanted to be an aeroplane pilot like his father or a balloon pilot.

Grandma eagerly welcomed them back on terra firma. 'I was worried about the balloon going too high in the sky and a bird pecking a puncture in the balloon,' she told them.

'Don't be so silly,' said Aunt Jemimah.

The balloonist offered to take Grandma up on his next flight but she politely declined, saying the thought of heights made her giddy.

Next day Aunt Jemimah had planned the biggest surprise of all - a trip to Ayers Rock - Uluru as it is called by the Aborigines. She told Nell and Jan that Uluru was probably the largest single rock in the world and that it was in the middle of the desert.

When they all arrived at their hotel at Ayers Rock the building looked as if it had sails and was sailing in the desert, so it did not surprise Nell to find it was called Sails in the Desert Hotel.

Outside Nell and Jan were impressed by the

tall eucalyptus trees - also called gum trees - with narrow green leaves.

'Grandma, those trees smell like your ointment you use in winter,' said Nell. Great Aunt Jemimah explained that eucalyptus tree oil is used all over the world for ointment and medicine.

After they had seen their hotel rooms the coach took the visitors on a tour to some strange colourful rocks called the Olgas.

'The man who discovered them named them after his wife, Olga,' explained Great Aunt Jemimah.

'If I discovered some rocks in a desert I'd call them the Nells!' said Jan.

'The local tribesmen call the rocks "Kota Tjuta", which means "many heads" in the Aboriginal language. There are 36 huge mysterious domes in those rocks,' continued Aunt Jemimah. They glowed bright orange in the sunshine close to, but as the coach drove further away they turned deep violet in colour. Nell hoped she could remember the colours to paint a picture of them for Grandpa.

The next exploit for them all would be the following morning, when they would witness the spectacular, wondrous sunrise at Uluru. They all had to go to bed early to be up at five o'clock in the morning for the coach to take them to the Rock.

99

CHAPTER FOURTEEN

An Outback Picnic

On leaving the hotel before dawn they all collected their packed breakfast boxes of ham and cheese, croissants, coconut cake and fruit juice and bottled water. Then the coach driver took them to the best viewpoint to view the legendary sunrise at Uluru with an Aboriginal native guide.

As the sun peeped over the horizon all the dogs in a nearby Aboriginal settlement began barking, as they do every day to wake up the sun.

Nell had never heard a canine choir before. 'They're much noisier than the seagulls and the seals back home,' she told Jan.

'They are loud, aren't they?' he agreed. 'I much prefer the tinkling of the cow bells in the Alps when Swiss cows greet the rising sun,' said Jan.

While they were standing quietly watching Uluru, the sky became paler and looked more blue as the sun rose. And the huge rock changed from a dark lump to a dusky orange colour which steadily became brighter and brighter with strong vertical shadows. As it got lighter Nell suddenly noticed a walnut-sized spider with very long legs in its web between the spinifex bush and the fence. It seemed as if the spider also wanted to greet the sun.

Nell wasn't sure that she liked spiders, certainly not such large ones. But the Aborigine guide told her that his own people respected all nature including spiders, who were useful and clever. Nell told him about the legend of the ancient Scottish King Robert the Bruce, who was taught by a spider in a Highland cave not to give up when he faced failure. The guide and Jan had never heard the legend and they wanted to hear more.

'Let me and Grandma tell you some more Scottish folk tales later,' promised Nell.

'And I can tell you the legend of William Tell and the boy with the apple on his head,' said Jan.

Then they all fell silent as they watched in

awe the spectacle before them.

Watching the ceremony of the sun's journey across the horizon over the Rock, Uluru, and up towards the heavens, Nell felt privileged. Most people in the world have never seen the glorious sunrise or sunset in the Scottish Hebridean Islands as well as on the other side of the world in the vast Australian outback.

As the sun climbed higher above Uluru in the blue cloudless sky the temperature also rose higher. Their guide took them to see some Aboriginal cave paintings and a mysterious pool that never dried up no matter how hot the sun burned in the furnace of the barren landscape.

Some tourists clambered over the Rock, the sacred Uluru to the Aboriginal people. Nell liked the Aborigines because they respected nature - the land and the animals - in the same way Nell was taught to respect the sea and marine life. She also respected their painting skills, boomerang throwing, didgeridoo music - but above all, their knowledge and love of nature.

CHAPTER FIFTEEN

Aborigines in The Desert

Although the tribesmen ate big plump witchity grubs, which are like white slugs, Nell did not think that was any worse than the overlanders and swagmen surviving on meat steaks of kangaroo, crocodile or camel. Nell and Jan both refused to eat the steaks as they preferred Australia's nut steaks and Australian fruit.

Nell and the Andersons met a group of tribesmen. They all got on very well, especially when Nell told them about Scotland and her great sea voyage across the world and Jan told them about their adventures with King Neptune when the ship crossed the Equator.

When they asked Nell her name she told them how she was also called 'The Child of the Wind' because of her travels like the sea breezes across the Oceans. The Aborigines laughed at this because they had named her 'The Child of the cold north land'. After Jan told them about Switzerland and the snow-covered high Alps and mountains, he was named 'The Boy of the White Mountains', but the Aboriginal desert people had never seen snow and they seemed to think it was like white leaves falling from trees in the clouds.

Each Aborigine who Nell met greeted her in his own language, 'Pukulpa pitjama Ananguku ngura Kutu', which Great Aunt Jemimah said meant 'Welcome to the Aboriginal land'. Nell replied with her Gaelic greeting of 'Ceud Mille Failte', which means 'a hundred thousand welcomes', while Grandma waved her sun hat at them. This pleased the tribesmen so much that they played the didgeridoo pipes for her.

'These didjees look like painted drainpipes and they sound like growling bears,' said Grandma.

'Grandma! They might not like it if they heard you say that. They've been ever so nice to us, and they offered to teach you how to play the didgeridoo.'

They all walked into the cultural centre together, where Grandma bought a carved wooden lizard as a paperweight for Grandpa.

'I'd like to buy him a didgeridoo!' said Great Aunt Jemimah.

'Oh no you don't!' said Grandma. 'It's already far too noisy when he plays the bagpipes.'

Aborigine Painting

Grandfather's present

CHAPTER SIXTEEN

Journey to Queensland

On their return to Alice Springs Airport the Andersons said their farewells to Jan and Frau Hesterberg. They exchanged addresses and promised to visit each other. Then the three generations of Andersons boarded a shiny silver Qantas aeroplane which had a large red kangaroo painted on its tail fin.

Grandma again overcame her reluctance for air travel as she and Nell were excited at the expectation of seeing Mother and Father's new home in Queensland. Even the 1,000 mile - or 1,500 kilometre - flight from Alice to Cairns, the gateway town to the great Barrier Reef, did not dissuade Grandma from another flight.

'As long as it is in an aeroplane with wings and engines and not a balloon with only hot air to keep it above the ground,' said Grandma.

Nell remembered the balloon flight with pleasure. But she agreed it would take a balloon days to glide across the sky northwards. And it might even be blown by the wind in the wrong direction out to sea or back into the outback desert instead of to Cairns. By plane it would take only a couple of hours, so they all sat back and relaxed in the plane, which was comfortable, if not so adventurous as a balloon.

When their plane landed in Cairns they arrived in a sub-tropical heat of 87°F in the middle of the hottest period from November to March. Nell's mother smiled with happiness and told Nell that Queensland had 300 sunny days a year, with over 7 hours of sunshine each day. And this was just one of these days.

'While Grandpa is back at home muffled up in his winter woolly coats and welly boots, here in Queensland everyone will be wearing sun hats, sandals and be covered with coats of sunblock,' Father told Grandma.

Grandma, who was a canny, thrifty old-fashioned Scots lady, exclaimed to Father, 'My word, good gracious! Aren't you lucky, Jack? You won't have to spend any money on coal and peat

fires to keep you warm.'

Mother laughed and replied, 'But here we certainly need air conditioning and fridges and freezers to keep everything cool.'

Grandma shook her head with puzzlement and murmured, 'Everything seems opposite in Australia from Scotland. We are up in the Highlands and you are down under. We are in the cold north and you are in the hot south. We have to wear woollies to keep us warm and you have to wear sun block to stop you burning.' The old lady shook her head again and said, 'I wonder what Grandpa will say when we tell him about all this.'

'Don't worry, Grandma,' said Nell, 'I shall write it all down in my diary for Grandpa, so he won't miss our news.'

Grandma said, 'Bless you, Nell. Grandpa will be so proud of you.'

The coach then arrived to take them from Cairns to Port Douglas by the Great Barrier Reef. As the Anderson family all climbed aboard the bus the driver welcomed them with the usual Aussie greeting, 'G'day, ladies and gents.' Then he added with a broad Aussie smile, 'With your accents you must be Scots. So welcome to Queensland and enjoy your stay.'

CHAPTER SEVENTEEN

Nell's New Home

They travelled along the Captain Cook Highway north to Port Douglas, which is the closest town to the Great Barrier Reef where Father had found a new job and Mother had found a new home and new friends and a new life in the beautiful little town.

Nell and Grandma had never seen more beautiful countryside and the most spectacular coastline. In less than an hour of travelling along the scenic highway, past golden sandy beaches and crystal clear coral sea, they arrived in Port Douglas.

Father and Mother proudly took Nell and Grandma to their new home. It was a glistening white painted wooden bungalow by the palm-fringed golden sands of Four Mile Beach.

Nell jumped up and down with excitement while Mother opened the door and welcomed Grandma and Nell into the little house. Grandma was tearful with happiness and said she wished Grandpa was also with them.

Then Grandma produced a black and white pebble from her handbag. She gave it to Mother and said, 'It's from our garden at home to remind you of our Island home in bonnie Scotland.'

Then she hugged Nell and said, 'This will be your new life and your new home until we return to Scotland.'

And that's what Nell decided she would call her next log-book for Grandpa - *Nell's New Life and New Home.*

Nell's New Life

- Book Four -

Nell arrives at her new family home in Australia, where Father and Mother have found a house by the white sands of Queensland at Port Douglas. It is a small town with its sunny face to the blue waters of the Coral Sea and the Great Barrier Reef and its back to the lush, cool, mysterious rainforests. Nell visits the tropical islands, sees underwater wonders and explores the dark green rainforests, meeting some of the strange creatures lurking there. She meets local schoolchildren and makes new friends called the Crew of Three, who get into trouble and make mischief.

CHAPTER ONE

Sun, Sand and Sea

When Nell woke up she took a deep breath and looked out of the window at her new home in Australia. She opened the window and took another deep breath of the gentle morning breeze, which was warmed by the bright sunshine outside.

She marvelled at Queensland's white sands at the end of her garden and the blue waters of the South Pacific Ocean washing gently over the coral of the Great Barrier Reef.

After a long pause she made her decision: This would be the first day of her New Life in her New Home in a New Country with New Friends.

What Nell felt about herself on the inside was not what people would see on the outside - she felt grown-up but still looked like a little girl. She would learn more than anyone expected.

She sat at the bedside table and opened her diary, the log-book that she wrote daily for her Grandpa back in Scotland. Nell penned at the top of the first page: 'My New Life'. She wrote as fast as she could because she could hear her Mother and Grandmother in the kitchen busily preparing breakfast, roasting piquant coffee beans and toasting sweet home-made honey bread.

Nell arrived last at the breakfast table.

Father and Mother each greeted her with the cheerful Aussie 'G'day, Nell'. Grandma, however, dourly muttered, 'If you sleep in again we'll eat your breakfast.'

'But I've been writing my log-book,' Nell protested. 'I didn't sleep in - but I forgot the time.'

Grandma frowned. 'Now we are down under on the other side of the world we must wake up with the dawn.' And, just to emphasize her Scottish habit of rising early, Grandma declared solemnly in Gaelic, 'Early to bed, early to rise, makes a lassie healthy, wealthy and wise.' Grandma then cast a stern glance for support at Mother, who quickly nodded agreement with the old lady.

But Father smiled and patted Nell on her shoulder and said in English, the language of Australia, 'Never mind, Nell. Our clocks here may be twelve hours behind Scottish clocks but you soon catch up with yourself.'

Everyone laughed and Mother said Grandpa back in Scotland would be having supper of Scotch broth and boiled fish while they were having breakfast of fresh fruit and toast.

'What a funny world it is!' muttered Grandma again. She liked talking and she liked even more to have the last word.

Nell's father, Jack, was like his father, Grandpa. He was a listener, not a talker. Father, like Grandpa, always encouraged and protected Nell. Father didn't enjoy writing - 'We're lucky to have Nell keep our travel log-book for us,' he declared.

Grandma smiled appealingly at Nell and said in quiet English, 'Can I read your diary, Nell?'

Nell looked at her. 'No,' she replied, 'my log-book is for Skipper Grandpa; he must read it first. It's my present to Grandpa.' Skipper is what the seamen and islanders at home called Grandpa.

Grandma stopped smiling. 'I hope you have written nice things about us to Skipper Grandpa,' she said.

Skipper Grandpa was Nell's best friend at home. She could tell him anything and never kept any secrets from him. When she was scolded for incorrect spelling or arithmetic by her schoolteacher, Miss Murray, Nell would tell Grandpa, who would explain how to avoid the mistakes in the future. And when she couldn't do her homework Grandpa was encouraging by explaining things to her. He said people could learn more from their mistakes than their successes if they did not repeat their mistakes.

As a young seaman Grandpa had sailed around the world and he was a very cosmopolitan, tolerant man. His great joy was reading travel books. He was proud when Nell promised to keep a log-book of her travels - just for him.

Grandpa was an old-fashioned ancient mariner who wore a sea captain's peaked cap and a seaman's navy blue jersey. His white beard made him look like Santa Claus and the Island boys called him Skipper Whitebeard. Over the years, he had taught many of the Island children boatmanship, sea safety and marine lore.

Like all old mariners, he liked telling yarns about the sea. He had his own sayings and phrases, such as 'People are like ships: some steer a straight course and others just drift with the tide, the crowd.' He would tell all the children crossing to the mainland on his Island ferry, 'If you don't know where you are going, you won't get there.'

He was so old-fashioned he called the radio 'the wireless' and he still preferred to write letters than to use what he called 'the telly-phone'.

Grandpa never allowed Grandma, Mother or Nell to clean the family's shoes. 'No mother or lassie in my family ever cleaned shoes or boots,' explained Grandpa, whose own father and grandfather had strong views about what was women's work, like managing the house, and what was men's work, like lifting and carrying. Back home on the Island, whenever Nell's shoes or boots got muddy Grandpa always cleaned and polished them so they were the brightest in the school. Some village boys teased Nell and called her 'Twinkle Toes' or 'Shiny Shoes'. But Grandpa cared for the shoes because he could not afford to buy new ones.

Now, in her New Life in a New Home in a

New Country, Nell decided she would be the 'Mistress of her own Destiny'. She would clean and polish her own shoes - she would prove to Skipper Grandpa and Father Jack she could be just as independent as a boy and 'steer her own course'. So after breakfast Nell got out the shoe box and said, 'Father - I'll polish the shoes and boots. You must not be late for work.'

Grandma and Mother looked astonished, lost for words in either Gaelic or English. But Father beamed with pride and said, 'Thank you, Nell. You are a big lass now in a big country.'

Nell hugged him and said, 'Yes, Father. And it's a new life.'

With that Father put on his seaman's boots, picked up his lunch box and went off to work on the Reef.

Grandma, Mother and Nell then cleared the breakfast table and washed the dishes - just before there was a loud knocking on their door. Standing outside was a tatty old man and a straggly lad.

CHAPTER TWO

Mr Mac and his Cabin Boy

The old man at the door looked like Rip Van Winkle who had just stepped out of an old history book. His long untidy white hair under a battered old straw hat was matched by a long white beard which covered his face except for two large blue eyes and a curved tobacco pipe. His faded navy blue shirt and trousers were ragged. He wore old sandals but you could not tell whether his brown feet were sun-tanned or just dirty. In Scotland he would have been called a scarecrow or a 'Touzie Tyke'.

In his brown gnarled hand he carried a big knobbly stick which he used as a door knocker. The old pipe had smelly smoke which made Nell cough.

The boy was thin and taller than Nell and about two years older. He had curly brown hair under his ragged straw hat and he wore an old T-shirt and shorts and no shoes. He reminded Nell of a scamp like Huckleberry Finn or Tom Sawyer, the Mississippi River boys she had read about in school. He was carrying a dead fish and a bamboo fishing rod in the other hand.

The old man and the skinny scamp both smelled of fish and the old man's pipe smelled like a rubbish bonfire.

Grandma, Mother and Nell stood in the doorway holding each other, too astonished by the two strange figures to move or speak.

Nell wanted to tell them to go away and take the dead fish with them, but she had been told not to speak to strangers - especially one with a big knobbly stick like the old man.

Mother moved her lips to speak but no words came out. Grandma pointed her finger at the white beard and was about to tell him to go away with the boy scamp and the fish when the bearded man roared with laughter. He shook his stick and waggled his beard when he lifted his battered straw hat and pulled the pipe out of his mouth. His loud voice boomed out in Gaelic, 'Ceud Mille Failte! A hundred thousand welcomes. Good

morning, ladies. We are honoured to welcome you to Queensland.'

Mother loosened her grip around Grandma and Nell. Grandma stepped forward, still pointing her finger at the stranger, and demanded of him. 'Who are you? What do you want here with all your noise and smelly pipe and fish and knobbly stick on our door? Off you go or I'll call the constable and have you put in prison.' All the time she was wagging her finger at the bearded man and speaking angrily in Gaelic. Nell had never heard Grandma so angry before, except when she and Grandpa caught a boat thief on the Island and took him to Oban, where the stern judge in a black gown and curly white wig sent the thief to prison.

The stranger tried to speak but Grandma grabbed his stick and told him, 'Don't interrupt me. Now off you go.'

The scamp looked scared of Grandma and he jumped away from the door with his smelly fish and tried to pull his grandfather with him. Grandma glowered at the boy and told him, 'Don't you bring any more smelly fish here. Do you understand English?'

The boy nodded and politely said, 'I'm

sorry, lady'.

Then the old white bearded man roared with laughter. He again raised his battered hat and bowed to Grandma. In his booming voice he said in Gaelic to Grandma, 'Greetings, Jeannie Anderson. Do you not remember me? I'm Angus MacSporran of Mull - your son Jack told me you were coming to Australia.' Then he added in English, 'This is no way to greet a Highland gentleman like me.' He straightened his hat and tried to look dignified.

Grandma looked even more astonished and exclaimed in English, 'Angus MacSporran from Tobermory! I don't believe it - after all these years - to meet you here! On the other side of the world. What a small world!'

Mr MacSporran again lifted his old hat and pushed his scared cabin boy forward to Grandma. 'This lad is my grandson Fergus - he's my cabin boy in my wooden shack and he's my first-mate on my boat. And he's the best fisherman in the port.' Mr Mac was very proud of the scamp.

Grandma said they had better come into the house and have a cup of tea - but not to bring the dead fish in the front door. Fergus said it was a

special barramundi fish which he had caught and brought as a welcome present. Grandma told Fergus to take it around to the kitchen back door because she didn't want it dropped on the nice carpet. She told Mr Mac to leave his smoky pipe outside.

Over cups of tea they all politely exchanged news again, after Grandma told Mr Mac not to speak so loud because she was not deaf. 'Stop that noise,' said Grandma. 'Is it outside you think you are in?' which Fergus didn't think was English.

Mr Mac explained that he and Fergus lived in a shack along the coast and they earned a living by fishing and painting boats. He had met Jack who told him to visit Grandma and Nell. Soon they were all exchanging stories and gossip. Grandma and Grandpa had gone to school in Oban with Mr MacSporran fifty years ago before he emigrated to Australia. Mrs MacSporran had died and Mr Mac and Fergus were alone in the world and only had each other to care for. The lad's parents had died in an accident when he was a small boy.

Fergus and Nell talked about their school and hobbies. Fergus explained that he could not speak Gaelic very well but he wanted to go to Scotland one day to see where his grandfather had grown up on the Island of Mull, off the west coast of Scotland. Nell had been there many times on school trips and family weekend visits and Fergus asked her lots of questions about the island.

Grandma said she was pleased to meet Mr MacSporran again and she would write to Grandpa back in Ellenabeich and tell him of their meeting. Mr Mac said she should tell Grandpa to come to Australia and Mr Mac would take him fishing and exploring with Fergus.

Grandma said she hoped they would all meet again soon.

CHAPTER THREE

Exploring the Port

Grandma and Nell were so curious about the town of Port Douglas that Mother took them on a walkabout in 'The Port', as the 3,000 local people call it.

A century ago it was a boom town during Australia's Gold Rush but when the gold ran out The Port became a sleepy, quaint town. It is also a major holiday spot for international tourists and backpackers who escape the cold winters in the northern hemisphere and Europe when Queensland is basking in sunshine, with an all year round superb climate.

The Port sits at the end of a palm-lined peninsula on a natural harbour which once was a busy port but now is more an old-fashioned picturesque fishing village than a town.

When Mother drove them in the family car into The Port they passed miles of cool, beautiful African oil palm trees, which make an exotic tropical entry to the town with its tree-lined streets.

It was hard for Nell to imagine that 100 years ago stage coaches and teams of horses and bullocks brought gold from the gold fields to The Port and shipped it around the world until a cyclone stormed along the coast and destroyed much of the town at the beginning of the twentieth century.

Mother explained that The Port is important because it is the closest point to the spectacular Great Barrier Reef, which is a colourful marine Garden of Eden. The Port also nestles between the paradise of the Reef and the serenity of the tropical rainforest coast.

Grandma and Nell enjoyed all the shops, old buildings and the Sunday market. Nell was most fascinated by the 'just caught' fish market, which had the greatest selection of fish and shellfish she had ever seen. The most prized fish is the barramundi, which is a delicacy and is hard to catch because it is a strong fighter. Among the multi-coloured fish were the coral trout, red emperors and mackerel as well as lots more - all from the deep blue waters off the coast.

While Grandma went sampling the restaurants and tea rooms, Nell and her mother went shopping for swim-gear, a scuba mask, flippers and a snorkel and an underwater camera for Nell to photograph the submarine life on the coral reef.

They also needed a lot of sunscreen to prevent sunburn because while Grandpa and everyone in Scotland were muffled up in their winter coats, in Queensland a coat of sunscreen is the only coat they wear in the sun. Even the young children are taught they must always wear sun hats as it is the law.

Grandma visited the district tourist office for a local map and she was so impressed with the service there that she booked different holiday expeditions. The first was a family trip on a paddle-steamer cruise with morning tea on a boat called the Lady Douglas. She also booked a train journey on an old sugar hauling locomotive engine called the Bally Hooley through the sugar cane fields to the sugar mill at Mossman, a few

Port Douglas

miles outside The Port.

There were so many other exciting excursions and trips to organize. Grandma said the whole family should visit the tourist office to arrange holiday trips. There was the wildlife centre, the butterfly farm, the crocodile park and Daintree rainforest and bungy jumping. They could also go on a boat trip to the Reef and excursions by submarine and glass-bottomed boat over the Reef to see the marine life.

Mother and Grandma had arranged so many adventurous outings that Nell would need to buy another diary log-book to record it all and report back to Grandpa. Meantime, Grandma was sending so many colourful picture postcards every day to Scotland to Grandpa and her friends that the Island postman would be very busy delivering them all.

Nell did all the family's washing up and polishing the car to earn some Australian dollars to buy postcards to send to her schoolfriends and Miss Murray, her teacher, who was following Nell's journeys on the big school map.

When the family returned home to the bungalow, over supper with Father, they all discussed a programme of events. Grandma wanted to take coach trips around the state of Queensland, especially an excursion on the scenic railway to Karunda, the village in the rainforest and Australia's tea plantation at the Nerada, as well as a visit to an Aboriginal settlement and the butterfly farm.

Mother wanted boat trips to the Reef in glass-bottomed boats and for snorkelling and diving. She insisted on a visit with Grandma to the butterfly farm to see the bright blue Ulysses butterfly, which Mother said is one of the most beautiful creatures in nature. Father disagreed and said he thought the most beautiful creatures lived on the Reef, such as the blue angel fish and the yellow butterfly fish. Grandma and Nell said they wanted to see them all.

Mother also wanted to take Nell and Grandma to the special aquarium in the nearby town of Townsville, which lets people see the wonderful marine life of the Reef. It gives the impression to visitors of being under water but not getting wet.

Grandma said she wan't sure if she could still swim in the sea as she hadn't done so for decades. But after visiting the aquarium and seeing the fish swimming behind the glass, Grandma said she would take up swimming again. But she would start by paddling on the beach before taking the plunge.

Since Mother had gone to Australia a year ago she had taken up snorkelling, scuba diving and deep diving to accompany Father on his hobby and work. She wanted to introduce Nell to the aqua exploration.

Now Grandma also wanted to visit the Reef and explore the small islands.

The Fish Market

CHAPTER FOUR

Mr Mac Goes Up in Smoke

After tea one evening, Father took the whole family for a walk, to promenade along the silver sands which curve along the palm-fringed Four Mile Beach to view the remarkably beautiful sunset.

The Four Mile Beach has always been called the Four Mile Beach and, although in Australia measurements are metric, it has never been called the 6.4 kilometre beach.

Walking along the four-mile-long sands, they met Mr Mac, as Nell called him, and his grandson Fergus, who were sitting on a tree log sorting out their fishing gear.

The old man was puffing on his pipe which smelled like burning tarry rope. When Grandma started coughing Mr Mac stopped smoking and quickly put his pipe away in his coat pocket.

Shortly after, Nell noticed smoke coming from Mr Mac's pocket. Just then the old man leapt up in the air in a cloud of smoke and jumped up and down slapping his burning pocket. He pulled out his pipe and ran down to the sea and splashed water on his smoking clothes.

Everyone, including Fergus, was laughing, except Mr Mac.

'Now, Angus,' Grandma said, 'you should know smoking is bad for your health - it's also dangerous.'

The old man just scowled and said he only put his pipe in his pocket in the first place because Grandma did not approve of smoking. Grandma scolded him in his own Gaelic language and said he had only himself to blame.

While all the adults were gossiping about the old country, Auld Scotia, Nell and Fergus discussed serious matters like where to swim safely, where there were reef 'nasties' in the water, like sharks, sea-snakes, stinging jellyfish and crocodiles, and where to get kayaks for canoeing.

'It can be dangerous swimming in tropical waters like these between the months of October and May because of the jellyfish like marine stingers and sea wasps. That's why they put up "stinger net" enclosures where it is safe to swim,' Fergus told Nell.

Fergus said the most exciting adventure he had had was bungy jumping at the Bungy Tower along the coast at Cairns. Nell had only seen bungy jumping on TV and thought it was the most dangerous exploit she had ever seen. But Fergus explained that the crazy sport was invented by Mr A J Hackett and is centred in a natural rainforest setting.

'It isn't any more dangerous than other sports, like paragliding, or mountaineering,' he said.

'No, I'm never going to go bungy jumping. I

don't care that there's never been an accident. You won't get me doing that even if Mr Hackett lets me go up the Tower for free,' replied Nell firmly.

Nell said she was more interested in learning the Australian language, which Australians call 'Strine'. So Fergus gave her quick answers to questions like:

Question: What is the outback or bush?

Answer: The Australian countryside outside cities.

Question: Billabong?

Answer: A water hole in a semi-dry river.

Question: Billy?

Answer: A container for making tea.

Question: Dingo?

Answer: Australian native dog .

Question: Swagman?

Answer: A vagabond, a tramp.

Nell asked Fergus if Mr Mac was a swagman.

'No, no,' he protested, 'Grandfather is a fair dinkum (a real, genuine) battler (which means he is someone who struggles for a living) to earn his tucker (food).'

Fergus told Nell that she was a 'Sheila', which is a female, while he said that his friend Billy Boy is a 'yahoo', which is an unruly person from the 'never never', the desert land far off in the outback.

Fergus asked Nell if Grandma was a 'sticky beak', which is a busy-body who likes bossing boys. Nell was shocked and indignantly replied that if he ever called Grandma a 'sticky beak' she would call him a 'yahoo' and not speak to him again.

Fergus looked downcast and replied, 'I'm sorry, Nell.' So she said, 'All right, let's stay friends and be polite to Grandma.' Fergus agreed and said he would catch a fair dinkum fish tomorrow for Grandma because she was a real lady and he wished he had a grandma like her.

CHAPTER FIVE

A Happy Reunion with Jan

As the glorious sunset coloured the shimmering sea and the unblemished beach, they all turned to walk back to the bungalow.

Mr Mac invited Grandma and Mother to visit him with Nell for afternoon tea the next time they were near his end of the beach.

'As long as you promise not to smoke that smelly pipe,' Grandma said.

'If you come I'll put on the billy for tea and give you some dinkum tucker,' said Fergus.

'What on earth is the lad talking about?' muttered Grandma. 'I hope it's not bad language.' Nell explained that Fergus was speaking Strine, which is Australians' talk.

As the family strolled home Nell asked Father why there were so many Scottish names, like Douglas, Cairns and Perth, in Australia, when the places didn't look Scottish at all. Father told her there were many English places as well because the first white men to settle in Australia were English and Scottish. Now Australia was one of the most cosmopolitan, international countries in the world, with people of every colour, religion and nationality living there.

'It's really a rainbow country with every colour from black Aborigines to white settlers and every one you can think of in between,' he said.

On arriving back at the bungalow they found a letter from Alice Springs. Frau Hesterberg had written to say that she and Jan were coming to Queensland for a holiday and would like to meet the Andersons again. Mother immediately phoned Frau Hesterberg and invited her and Jan to stay at the bungalow for a month.

A few days later the Swiss boy and his mother arrived. There was another happy reunion with a special barbecue and a musical evening which the Scots call a ceilidh.

Grandma played the piano and Mr Mac played the fiddle and Jan, Nell and Fergus were allowed to stay up late into the night with the adults. Grandma and Mr Mac also sang Scottish songs and Father and Fergus sang 'Waltzing Matilda' while Frau Hesterberg and Jan sang Swiss folk songs about snow-covered Alps and the bears of Berne.

At the end of the evening, the Scots all sang the traditional Scottish parting song called 'Auld Lang Syne', which made Grandma weep because she was thinking of poor Grandpa back in cold Scotland all on his own. Jan was puzzled and asked Nell and Fergus why Scots people sang songs that made them cry instead of smile.

Over the next week Nell, Fergus and Jan became inseparable - they washed the dishes and

polished Father's car together and they helped Mr Mac to tidy his garden and paint his shed. They also did the shopping in the market for the adults. All this 'The Trio', as they were called by the Port people, did together. The trio themselves preferred to call themselves the 'Crew of Three'.

When Fergus had his eleventh birthday, his grandfather gave him an old rowing boat as a present. The Anderson family gave him a new fishing rod and Frau Hesterberg and Jan gave him one of Jan's new Swiss T-shirts which had a picture of the Alps on it.

The old boat badly needed painting, and Fergus taught Nell and Jan how to mix the paint and brush it on. When they finished and returned home, Grandma complained that the Crew had painted themselves more than the boat and she made them all wash before they could have their meal.

The next day, after the boat paint had dried, Nell suggested the boat be launched at the beach and officially named. It would have to be splashed on the bows with lemonade because they didn't have a bottle of champagne, like a queen or a president does when launching a ship.

'But it's got to have a name,' said Jan. 'Why don't we name the boat the Sea Arrow?'

Fergus suggested 'Rover', but Nell said that sounded more like a pet dog. Nell looked at the newly painted boat and said, 'Why don't we call the boat Triton?'

Fergus looked up at Nell and said, 'What's that?'

Nell explained: 'Triton was the son of Neptune who makes the oceans roar by blowing through a sea shell.'

Fergus looked thoughtful and hesitated. Then he said, 'I don't think I like Triton. I don't want to hear the oceans roar - when the seas are angry there is trouble. I think we will give the boat a better name,' said Fergus. 'We will call her the Lady Nell,' he said gallantly. Jan clapped his hands in agreement. Nell blushed with embarrassment and could only say, 'Thank you, Fergus. You are very kind.'

So they splashed the bows with the bottle of lemonade and as Fergus and Jan pushed the boat into the water, Nell said solemnly, 'May God bless and protect all who sail in her.' Then they all rowed the boat around the bay.

CHAPTER SIX

Mr Mac and the Bodach

O ften Mr Mac came to the beach to sit on the rock in the cool shade of the palms. The Crew of Three liked to hear his sea stories and yarns. Occasionally he taught the trio to sing sea shanties and pirate songs.

Jan especially wanted to learn more about the seas because in Switzerland they were taught more about mountains and the Alps instead of the oceans. He wanted to know the difference between the seas and oceans. Mr Mac stroked his beard and sucked on his pipe but did not light the tobacco and smoke in case Grandma saw him in a cloud of grey smoke and scolded him again.

'Oceans,' said Mr Mac, 'are huge masses of water covering more than half the world. Oceans separate the continents like the Atlantic and Pacific. Oceans separate Europe and America or Asia and Australia. A sea is part of an ocean, like the Seven Seas, such as the North Sea in the Atlantic and the South Seas in the Pacific.'

Jan also wanted to know the difference between a ship, a boat, a liner and a craft. Mr Mac produced a little English dictionary from his pocket and gave it to Jan and suggested the Swiss lad look up the words and learn to use the dictionary.

While Nell and Fergus helped Jan to find the words in the little book, Mr Mac read his newspaper. When they had all stopped reading, Mr Mac explained to the curious trio how the world seemed to grow smaller as he grew older.

'The circumference of the world - that's how far it is all the way round - is about 25,000 miles. When I was a boy it seemed a miracle for anyone to travel by train, balloon or ship around the world in 40 days, but now aeroplanes can fly passengers in comfort around the world in 40 hours. It took me weeks to sail on an emigrant ship from Scotland to Australia when I was a young man. Now I could fly to Scotland in less than a day, if I could afford it.'

When the two boys ran out of questions for Mr Mac, he pulled his pipe from his pocket and put it to his mouth. When everyone was quiet, Nell asked Mr Mac if he knew anything before he left Scotland about the Gaelic spirit of the sea, the Bodach Na Mara.

Mr Mac's blue eyes twinkled, he stroked his white wiry beard and pocketed his pipe. Then he sighed and said quietly, 'Och, the Bodach, the Bodach Na Mara,' and he slowly nodded his head and looked far out to sea. It seemed his thoughts were far away - as if he was a boy again back in the auld country, back in his native Hebrides on the Western Isles of Scotland, half a world and a whole lifetime away.

Fergus gently touched his Grandfather's arm and held it tenderly. Nell had never seen such a big boy being so gentle with a man.

'Are you all right, Grandfer?' he asked quietly. Fergus only called the old man 'Grandfer' when they were alone and Nell had never heard it before.

Mr Mac didn't move. Nell thought his thick white hair and white beard looked like the white crest of the Atlantic roller waves. Jan thought it looked like a snow-topped mountain in the Alps.

But Fergus thought Mr Mac was far away across the Ocean.

'What do you see, Grandfer?' the lad asked. Still the old man did not move. But in his slow deep Scottish voice, which still did not have an Australian accent, Mr Mac murmured in Gaelic, 'The Bodach. How could I forget the Bodach and my home, my island, the grey rocks, the seals swimming in the long kelp in the waves and the westerly winds beating the North Sea, the home of the Bodach?'

His voice sounded deeper and slower as if it was coming from the still ocean deeps far below the restless waves. 'Nach Uramach an Cuan,' he whispered. 'How worthy of honour is the sea.' The old man's blue eyes were watering and he blinked and pretended the sun was shining in his eyes as he wiped away the tears with his rough knotty hand.

Fergus put his hand on his grandfather's shoulder and whispered, 'I'm here, Grandfer. I'm with you.'

Jan and Nell watched silently without moving or speaking.

Fergus turned to Nell and said, 'I don't have all his Gaelic. Please tell me what Grandfather said.' Nell said she would tell him later. The old man was sitting unmoved on the boulder, just as Nell remembered the Bodach sitting on the rock in the sea outside her home in the Hebridean Islands.

Then, slowly, Mr Mac reached for his pipe and lit the tobacco and blew out a little blue smoke.

'Nach Uramach an Cuan,' he repeated.

'Yes, yes,' said Nell. 'How worthy of honour is the sea.' She added quickly, 'Whoever honours the sea will be honoured.'

Mr Mac stroked his beard again and in his

deep rumbling voice said, 'So you have seen the Bodach, Nell?'

The girl nodded and said in Gaelic, 'Yes, my Grandpa and I both know the Bodach.'

The two boys sat down beside Nell and Mr Mac. 'How do you know the Bodach, Nell?' asked Fergus.

So she narrated to them the Gaelic folk tale of the Bodach and her own story as it had been written in her first story, 'The Old Man of the Seas', and her own sea voyage across the oceans in her log book 'Child of the Wind'.

When she ended her story, Mr Mac said, 'And, you know, children, the Bodach Na Mara is in all the seas and oceans and his message to honour the sea is more important than ever before. We must all care for the sea.'

CHAPTER SEVEN

Fergus Remembers the Deadly Storm

So Nell told Mr Mac that's why she wanted to be a marine biologist. Fergus was wide-eyed with surprise. 'A what?' he asked.

'A marine biologist, a scientist who studies the sea and marine life,' replied Nell quietly but firmly.

Fergus shook his head doubtfully. But Mr Mac complimented Nell and said he was sure she would one day be a sea scientist because he could see that she loved the sea and sea life.

Jan said he wasn't sure if he wanted to be an airline pilot like his father or a balloonist to travel the world. He asked Fergus what he wanted to be.

Fergus looked embarrassed, hung his head and looked sad.

'Come on, tell us,' said Nell.

Fergus looked up at the sky in the same wondering manner as when his grandfather had looked out to sea and talked of the Bodach.

After a pause Fergus said he wanted to be a meteorologist, to study the weather and forecast any cyclones that sometimes struck Queensland and caused terrible damage to the coast, the forests and farmlands. He seemed quiet and thoughtful until his grandfather said it was time to go home. Later her father told Nell that Fergus's mother and father had died in a cyclone storm which struck the coast when he was a baby. It was then that Nell understood why Fergus had not wanted to name his boat Triton, the son of Neptune who makes the oceans roar.

As they walked together, Jan said to Nell, 'In Switzerland we honour the spirits of the mountains. I didn't know the spirit of the seas was everywhere in all the oceans.' He also said Nell should be honoured that Fergus wanted to name his boat the Lady Nell.

When they arrived home there was an appetizing aroma of home baking throughout the house.

At tea, Nell and Jan were thinking of Fergus

and Mr Mac having their simple meal of damper and boiled fish. So they were delighted when Grandma announced that she, Mother and Frau Hesterberg had spent the afternoon baking cakes. Tomorrow they were going to take a picnic box of home baking to Mr Mac and Fergus. The three ladies explained how Grandma had baked Scottish scones, Frau Hesterberg had made a Swiss chocolate cake and Mother had made a box

of butter shortbread.

Father said he hoped he would also be able to take some to work with him, and Nell said she would like some Swiss chocolate cake and Jan asked if he could try some shortbread and cakes.

'We'll see - it depends if you behave yourselves,' said Grandma with a mischievous smile. 'You will both have to cut the lawn for Father.'

CHAPTER EIGHT

Jan and Fergus Make Mischief

The next day the household were all up early to be ready in their best clothes for the Sunday morning service.

Grandma missed the church service at home and singing the hymns, so she insisted that they all go to the church to give thanks for their safe voyage halfway around the world.

Nell looked very smart in her bright white dress with tartan hair ribbon. Jan was dressed in his best lederhosen, leather trousers and white shirt. On the way to church they joined up with Mr Mac, who had combed his long hair and beard and was wearing sandals. Fergus was wearing clean brown shorts and Jan's Swiss T-shirt.

While the adults were all talking together Jan and Fergus were busy chatting and whispering together.

Nell had warned Fergus that Jan was a prankster who enjoyed practical jokes, like putting a plastic frog in Mr Mac's fish tank and squirting the hosepipe water at the neighbour's pet dog, who chased Jan to get a shower in the hot sun.

At the church it was all very solemn and proper. The minister, the Reverend Mr Black, welcomed the Andersons and Hesterbergs to the congregation. Grandma, Mother and Nell wore their best Sunday hats with ribbons and plastic cherries and white gloves. Jan and Fergus were sitting in the pews behind them. They appeared quite respectable with combed hair and clean shirt collars. But they looked naughty with their heads together and whispering to each other.

Nell decided it was not ladylike to turn around to watch them so she ignored them and read her hymn book instead. She was delighted that the first hymn was her favourite. Everyone stood up when the elderly, staid organist, Miss Philomena Plunkett, began playing the music and everyone sang 'All things bright and beautiful'. The music and singing grew louder. 'All creatures great and small...' Then the lady organist suddenly

plonked her hands on the keys, shrieked and ran over to the little choirmaster, Mr Crump.

'There's a mouse, a mouse in the organ,' she gasped. Mr Black, the minister, calmed her down and asked everyone to continue singing until Miss Plunkett composed herself again and the choir boys caught the mouse.

Nell turned around and saw Jan and Fergus trying to hide their heads below the top of the pews. The lads were looking their usual mischievous selves instead of looking concerned for the welfare of the distressed Miss Plunkett or helping the choir boys catch the mouse.

Grandma turned to Mother and said she would not come back to church until the mouse was caught. Frau Hesterberg said the minister should keep a cat in the church or have a collection for money to buy mousetraps.

The choirmaster walked over to the organ and to gasps of admiration from some trembling ladies in the congregation, the brave little choirmaster picked up the mouse and put it in his pocket.

Miss Plunkett looked adoringly at Mr Crump, who escorted her back to her seat. She looked nervously around until Mr Crump nodded reassuringly to her. Then she sat down and started playing the music again and everyone resumed singing 'All things wise and wonderful, the Lord God made them all'. Everyone, that is, except Jan and Fergus.

After the service ended and the congregation left their pews and filed noisily out of the church door, Nell noticed the two lads had hurried out first before Mr Black got to the door. They were outside, hiding behind a big gravestone while the minister greeted the worshippers as they filed out and said their farewells.

Mr Crump, the hero of the occasion, held up the mouse for everyone to see. The devout ladies of the congregation looked admiringly at their hero. Then the minister held the mouse up by the tail. It was only a toy clockwork mouse. Miss Plunkett looked abashed and all the ladies chattered and said how disgraceful it was that someone should play such a trick in the House of God which

Grandma calls a kirk. Frau Hesterberg and Mother nodded agreement when Grandma said that such a troublesome wicked person who imported a mouse into the kirk should be punished for their impudence.

Nell looked in the graveyard again and watched Jan and Fergus blushing and guiltily holding dirty handkerchiefs to hide their faces as they also tried to hide behind each other and the gravestone. She remembered what Jan had done before with his trick plastic frog and the trick black rubber spider.

137

- CHAPTER NINE -

The Three Wise Monkeys

Following Grandma and Mother, Nell adjusted her hat, fingered her white cotton gloves just like Grandma and sniffed haughtily. Then she walked past the two guilty lads and ignored them as if she did not know them. At the church gate Grandma announced that whoever was responsible for such wickedness as upsetting the lady organist with such an unrighteous trick in the Lord's kirk should be ashamed of themselves. They should be ordered by the Magistrate to wash the church floors and cut the grass in the graveyard.

Jan's mother nodded agreement and Mr Mac said the culprits should be made to walk the plank. The two boys shifted their feet, blushed and blew their noses again with their handkerchiefs.

Nell decided that she did not want to be in the Crew of Three with such pranksters. She would not speak to them again. And she kept her vow not to talk to them - that is until the next day when the two lads invited her down to the beach to join them in the rowing boat with their fishing rod. She

said she would reluctantly accompany them as long as they promised no more tricks in the kirk. Both boys eagerly promised. They begged her not to tell the minister, because their gang motto was 'All for one and one for all'. Nell only agreed if they added to their crew motto to 'Hear no evil; see no evil; speak no evil' like the motto of the three wise monkeys. The chastened lads reluctantly agreed and shamefacedly recited their new motto after Nell.

All of them then got into the boat and Nell told the boys to row properly and behave themselves. She had again put the two bigger boys in their place. They were more scared of her than they would admit. They knew that the church floor was very large and the graveyard grass and weeds were long and thick. And they didn't want to upset Grandma and Mr Mac as well as Nell.

When the sun became too hot to go out fishing or painting the boats by the jetty, the trio sat in the shade under the palm trees.

Fergus taught them to speak some more 'Strine' with such words as 'BYOG', which means 'bring your own grub', which is how he hinted to Nell and Jan to bring some of Grandma's shortbread and Frau Hesterberg's chocolate cake when they were fishing. Because he was taller than Nell, Fergus called her a 'nipper', which is Strine for a small child. She replied that she would call him a 'skinnymalink', which is Scots for a skinny boy. Jan said it was a rule of the Crew of Three not to call each other names except chum, shipmate or pal. He said he didn't want to be in the 'Crew of Yahoos' and he would resign if they did not stop arguing. The trio held hands and recited their crew motto, 'All for one and one for all' and ran down the beach to swim in the sea, which was like a warm bath. Nell also told Fergus that she was honoured that he wanted to name his boat the Lady Nell.

When they returned to the shade of the palm tree Jan taught them how to use a 'hand sundial' to tell the time. He also explained how to use a watch as a compass in case they were ever lost at sea.

Fergus liked Nell to tell him about Scotland and her Island home and school. He said it would be fun to walk in the Scotch mist and gentle rain, instead of the blistering heat or monsoon rains of Australia. He was also very curious about Switzerland and how Jan went skiing in the Alps and had snowball fights at school. Most of all, Fergus wanted to go on a toboggan ride and climb the Matterhorn, and be the first Aussie to plant the Blue Southern Cross flag to fly on its summit. Jan was amazed that Fergus had never seen snow, or realized how cold Europe was in winter.

'But, in Europe at least,' said Nell, 'we don't get cyclones or monsoon rain.'

CHAPTER TEN

Fergus and Jan in More Trouble

One morning Grandma asked the family to finish their breakfast quickly because, with Mother and Frau Hesterberg, she would be busy all morning and afternoon baking scones, shortbread, Swiss cakes and jam for the local Ladies Home Baking Competition.

The next day, when all the ladies stood behind their trestle tables while the judges were sampling the goodies, Nell, Jan and Fergus were sitting under the stage, also sampling a trayful of cakes, which Fergus' friend Billy Boy had brought in from one of the tables.

Billy Boy said he would share the goodies if they would let him join the Crew of Three. Fergus said they would think about it. Nell asked if he had stolen the tray, but Billy Boy replied that the goodies were for helpers and he had helped himself. Nell said she wouldn't eat any more and, with the help of Jan and Fergus, pushed Billy Boy from under the stage.

The doorman saw him and the Ladies Committee all grabbed the Crew of Three and Billy, who still had jam and crumbs on their chins. As a punishment Nell and the three boys were ordered to help the Ladies Committee to wash all the dishes and trays and sweep the hall floor under the watchful supervision of Grandma and the grim caretaker. The Crew of Three told Billy Boy he would never be allowed to join their Crew now he had made them suffer such indignity as washing up in the hall kitchen.

CHAPTER ELEVEN

Sooty upsets Grandma

Mr Mac invited the Andersons, and Jan and his mother, to visit his wooden shack for afternoon tea next Sunday. Grandma, Mother and Frau Hesterberg decided to take a selection of Scots delicacies of shortbread, oatcakes and cake for the old man and his grandson.

When they arrived, the shack had been tidied up, and clean newspapers put on the table as a tablecloth. Mr Mac had also polished his old silver teapot and Fergus had put away all their fishing gear and bits and bobs. Mr Mac insisted that Grandma sit in the best chair and Mother passed around the cake and shortbread while Frau Hesterberg served tea in the mugs, which Grandma said were not as nice as proper cups and saucers.

She pulled out her knitting bag, which she often took around with her, and took out a large ball of wool and knitting needles. While Mr Mac was entertaining them all with sea yarns, Grandma dropped the ball of wool on the floor.

Suddenly, a big black cat shot out from under the sofa chair and started playing with the ball of wool. Grandma tried to catch the ball of wool, and Mr Mac tried to catch the sooty black cat. But Sooty seemed to think it was all a game, and rolled the wool under the chairs and around the table legs.

Grandma was shouting in Gaelic at Mr Mac to catch the cat, while Nell and Mother were trying to unravel the wool. Jan and Fergus just stood there gobbling more cakes and giggling at the antics.

Eventually, the cat was caught and the tangled wool given back to Grandma. She put away her knitting needles and told Mr Mac that he should properly train the big black cat not to cause trouble.

'I had been trying to knit you a pair of socks,' she told him, 'but now that your cat has ruined the knitting you will have to buy your own socks.'

'I'm sorry, but Sooty is a good mouser.

Anyway,' he said, lifting up his bare foot, 'I don't wear socks, even in the winter - it's never cold enough here to need them.'

Grandma looked at his foot and said he should wash it more often, or wear socks to cover his muddy feet. With that she closed her knitting bag, stood up and marched out with the two ladies and the Crew of Three following her like a procession.

Mr Mac was left standing at the door, lighting his pipe.

'Thank you for the afternoon tea,' he said and in he went to eat up all the shortbread and oatcakes, which were the best he had ever eaten since he left Scotland half a century ago. When Fergus returned there was only one biscuit and one cake left for him and Mr Mac was sound asleep in his armchair, with the black cat purring on the old man's chest.

CHAPTER TWELVE

The Big Fish Supper

*I*t was a whole week before Mr Mac and Grandma met again at the church service and talked to each other. He apologised to Grandma in his best and most polite Gaelic and pleaded with her not to be angry with him.

'Och, Jeannie Anderson,' he said, 'you make the best shortbread and oatcakes outside bonnie Scotland. You are a bonnie cook - and I haven't got anyone else to talk to with the Gaelic. Can we not be friends again? I'll bring you a big barramundi to cook.' Grandma looked down at his feet, which looked clean, and she noticed he had combed his hair and beard.

'Well, well, Angus MacSporran of Mull,' sniffed Grandma, 'I shall think about it. But you will have to bring a good fish for the supper next Saturday night, when you come with Fergus.' And she said in a louder voice, 'Don't you bring your big black cat with you when

you come to my house.'

Mr MacSporran smiled and held on to his pipe and tobacco in his pocket. 'Of course, Jeannie Anderson,' he said, 'and will we get more oatcakes and shortbread on Saturday?'

Grandma was walking away and did not reply. When she had turned the corner, he put his pipe to his mouth and lit the tobacco.

'Och,' he said to Fergus, 'we'll keep out of trouble and catch a bonnie barramundi for Saturday night.' And grandfather and grandson walked home to their shack thinking about the feast they hoped to get at Grandma Anderson's on Saturday. Grandfer Mac turned to Fergus and said in a whisper, 'I would even stop smoking and throw my old pipe away for a plate of Jeannie Anderson's Scotch broth.'

Fergus just hoped he would get a plate of Grandma's apple pie and custard. Together they planned to catch a big fish for Grandma.

CHAPTER THIRTEEN

Nell Makes More Friends

Although it was school holidays, Mother and Frau Hesterberg decided that Nell and Jan should not neglect their education. So arrangements were made for educational trips and for Nell and Jan to visit the local library to read about Queensland, the Great Barrier Reef, the rainforests and the Aborigines.

At the library a very helpful lady, Miss White, was delighted to meet the Scots lass and the Swiss boy and she liked answering their questions. She was even more pleased that they brought Fergus, a local boy, with them, because he had not often used the local library and had not known what he had missed.

The Crew of Three were soon bombarding Miss White with questions, which seemed to make her happier the more difficult they were. Fergus whispered to Nell that it would be a great place to do his homework after the school holidays were over - especially as the librarian knew where to find all the answers to difficult questions. Miss White was not a 'sticky beak' but a dinkum lady. Jan said he would learn English quicker here than at home, although the Strine words like billabong, dinkum and sticky beak are as strange as some Scots words, like 'aye' for 'yes', 'bonnie' for 'good' and 'haggis' for a strange meal. Billy Boy didn't come to the library, but they often met local children like Dolly Cook, Sally Wren and Fearless Freddy, who wasn't afraid of mice or spiders, and Pixie Peter, who had pointed ears.

Nell invited them all over to the bungalow for a Saturday afternoon picnic - and when Fergus told them about Grandma and Frau Hesterberg's shortbread and cakes, they all said they would be there. The librarian said she would like to come too but she had to work sorting out

all the library books.

'Never mind,' said Nell. 'We'll bring you a box of Grandma's shortbread to have with your morning tea.' And Jan promised her a piece of Swiss cake if Fergus, Billy Boy, Fearless Freddy and Pixie Peter didn't eat it all at the picnic.

CHAPTER FOURTEEN

The Dark Forest

However, Grandma decided it would be more interesting to have a picnic in the rainforest. She arranged with Fearless Freddy's father, who owned a motor coach, to hire the bus to take them all inland to the lush, green forest.

People think of Australia as a dry land of arid desert outback, but it is also a land of wet tropics and unspoiled cool, green rainforests, which is the complete opposite of the Queensland coast and the Great Barrier Reef.

The librarian had explained to the trio that Queensland is the place where two diverse world heritage eco-systems - the Reef and the rainforest - meet. And they are protected for ever for future generations of the world's children.

On the bus journey, they passed rivers and streams with the Red Triangle signs painted with crocodile heads. Fergus explained that the signs warned people not to swim in the waters because there were man-eating crocodiles there.

In the forests they saw giant, two-foot-high flightless cassowary birds. Even Fearless Freddy was scared of the funny-looking birds because he said they chased people and used their long, strong legs for kicking. Everyone stayed in the bus until the big birds walked away. But they all got out again to see the tree-climbing kangaroos and to have the picnic where they could watch the crystal clear streams tumble over waterfalls and deep gorges.

The party all kept together because the cassowary birds might come back, and because all the strange, tropical birds in the tropical trees were making very frightening noises. Nell was disappointed not to see koala bears or even a platypus, or a jabiru stork, which is the state emblem of Queensland. But she didn't want to see crocodiles or snakes.

Everyone had such an enjoyable picnic, and there was no trouble between Fearless Freddy, Billy Boy and Pixie Peter, because they did not want to upset Grandma. And Fergus, Jan and

Nell said if they behaved themselves they could go on the next picnic to the Barrier Reef. So they were all very polite to Grandma, Mother and Frau Hesterberg, who had made such a good picnic. On the way home the Crew of Three and their friends all sang. 'For she's a jolly good fellow' to Grandma, and also sang 'Waltzing Matilda' with the bus driver until a policeman stopped the bus to warn the driver of cassowary birds and crocodiles crossing the road.

Grandma, Mother and Frau Hesterberg told the driver to make sure the bus doors were closed to keep the wild animals, giant birds and snakes out of the bus. Fearless Freddy told Grandma not to worry. 'Have no fear, Freddy's here,' he said, but Pixie Peter sat behind Grandma for safety with Dolly Stone and Sally Wren.

When they arrived back at the bungalow late at night, Father and Mr Mac were making plans for the next exciting excursion by the group to the Great Barrier Reef.

BEWARE CASSOWARIES CROSS REGULARLY NEXT 10 KM

CHAPTER FIFTEEN

A Trip to the Reef

A week later, when everyone had recovered from their expedition to the rainforest, the party gathered at the harbour for a day trip to the Reef. No one was allowed on the boat unless they had a sun hat and T-shirt and sunblock because of the fierce sunshine out on the waters.

The cruise boat skipper Captain Storm was a friend of Father's and Mr Mac's and he gave a welcome speech and a short talk about Queensland's 4,000 kilometres of coast and the 2,000 miles-long Reef. He explained that the Reef is one of the seven wonders of the world and that it can be seen from the moon as a white line in the blue sea. It is seven times larger than Britain. It is also the largest structure ever made by living creatures. The best way to see the Reef is very close up by snorkelling, scuba diving or from a glass-bottomed boat. It is just as interesting looking at the coral and the marine creatures with a microscope as with a telescope or from an aeroplane.

When Captain Storm ended his interesting Welcome Aboard Talk, Nell and all the other passengers put on their life jackets before the engine of the cruise boat roared into life and it headed out of the harbour straight for the open seas towards the Great Barrier Reef, which is made up of nearly 3,000 separate islands.

On the way the boat anchored at the Low Isles between the Port and the Reef itself. The isles are coral islets with glistening white beaches and coconut palms. The warm shallow waters shimmer like a protective canopy to shield the dazzling coral garden with its multi-coloured corals and shells of all shapes and sizes and a kaleidoscopic array of technicolour sea life in the underwater paradise.

That is why swimming with flippers is better than walking over the coral. Billions of tiny sea creatures in the Reef attract millions of fish of every size and colour swimming in the garden of corals of every colour and shape instead of flowers in a garden on land.

The Reef was discovered two centuries ago by

Captain James Cook, the explorer who made his perilous voyage all the way from England to Australia in a small wooden ship. Nowadays, most of the islands are deserted except for visiting scientists, swimmers and divers.

As the modern luxury boat took Nell and the group towards the isles, Nell was delighted to learn that there was a young lady who was a marine biologist on board. It was her job to give a talk to the passengers and explain the wonders of the sea and the hundreds of different kinds of colourful kaleidoscopic fish living in this underwater Garden of Eden. She explained that coral reefs take thousands of years to grow and are built by multitudes of little animals called polyps, which make limestone. So everyone must be careful not to damage the delicate structures by walking on the coral.

It was possible for Grandma and Mr Mac, along with elderly passengers and small children who couldn't swim, to see the coral and reef creatures close up in the comfort of the underwater observatory without getting their feet wet. From inside the hull of the cruise boat they could watch the marine life and fish feeding on the sea plants.

151

CHAPTER SIXTEEN

Floating with the Sea Creatures

After the marine biologist Miss Morris gave her informative talk, which she illustrated with pictures and photographs, she took Nell and other passengers, under the supervision of a swimming instructor, on a snorkelling tour of the coral waters. Snorkelling is swimming with a face mask and a breathing tube.

Miss Morris and the instructor Mr Mason explained that the coral waters and the Reef are Australia's special natural treasures. The Reef is the largest marine park in the world. And to protect the delicate coral and marine creatures there must not be any spear fishing by swimmers and divers.

Nell and her friends, Fergus, Jan, Fearless Freddy, Dolly, Pixie Peter and Sally Wren, were each properly taught swimming and snorkelling with all the equipment of flippers, face mask and snorkel.

As the boat's crew, Miss Morris and Mr Mason took Nell and her friends swimming in the crystal clear waters of the marine wonderland, everyone was surprised at how easy it was to learn snorkelling from the helpful instructors.

While she swam over the yellow and pink sunshine coral, Nell watched through her face mask and breathed through the snorkel and it was like gliding on the water. She watched the blue and orange striped harlequin fish and the pink coral fish resting in the coral. The magnificent blue angel fish were so close that she could touch them.

In the water, men and women, boys and girls are all equal. It is not physical strength but intelligence, skill and experience that are most important. Nell realized that she could swim as well as the bigger boys and she was especially careful and attentive and kept close to Miss Morris.

As she floated on the water, safe in this special place, Nell was proud that her father Jack was helping the scientists and biologists in the marine park and that Father was working to protect the coral reefs and conserve the fragile marine life. She hoped that one day there would be a similar marine

park in Scotland and that she, her Father and Grandpa Anderson could all help at a Scottish marine park.

While she swam among the fish and sea creatures, Nell was sure that the ancient Gaelic Old Man of the Seas, the Bodach Na Mara, would approve and watch over the marine park and its purpose, for it would be following the Bodach's message to the world: 'Whoever honours the sea shall be honoured'.

Captain Storm and Miss Morris were proud of the Reef marine park, which they said was honoured all over the world as well as in Australia. It was the result of the dreams of the Queenslanders and of the choices they had made. As Miss Morris told Nell in her talk, 'We are free to dream but our dreams are not free. We have to study, learn and work to make our dreams come true. There is nothing to stop other countries supporting marine parks.'

And all that is true, thought Nell, as she swam below the water in the submarine gardens and coral rockeries with the astonishing variety of creatures and plants.

Pearl Oysters and Giant Clams

Clown fish played hide and seek in the sea anemones. Nell decided she would try to count the different creatures and plants, the pearl oysters, tiny cowrie shells and giant clams and the coral cod and monster fish which gobbled up small fish. While Nell was admiring the sponges, the sea squirts and cuttlefish, some brightly coloured butterfly fish danced around her until a shoal of barracudas flashed past her.

Nell wanted to see the dolphins but instead saw huge manta rays that floated past her like giant triangular kites.

All the time Nell and her friends were below the water swimming among the fish, Grandma and Mr Mac and the other passengers were also enjoying themselves, watching the coral and the fish world from a glass-bottomed boat that had joined the cruise boat. It was all so interesting that time passed very quickly and Captain Storm soon announced that everyone had to return to the cruise boat for the voyage back to Port Douglas.

After the crew tied up the boat in the harbour, Captain Storm bade everyone farewell and hoped they would all return again. Mr Mac asked all the passengers to give three cheers for Captain Storm and his crew. Grandma asked all the children to give three cheers for Miss Morris and Mr Mason for teaching the youngsters so much. The children cheered so loudly that Grandma put her hands over her ears.

Over the next few weeks Mother took Nell and Grandma back on the cruise boat for day excursions to the Reef. Everyone applauded Grandma when she went swimming with Mother and Nell on the white beach at Low Island. Mr Mac took photographs of Grandma, Mother and Nell swimming together to send back to Grandpa in Scotland.

Before Jan and Frau Hesterberg finished their holiday in The Port to return to Alice Springs, Mr Mac took them fishing in his own fishing boat with Fergus, who caught a big barramundi fish. They proudly carried the big fish to a local restaurant where the chef in his tall white chef's hat and smart white overall cooked the barramundi for their supper that night.

Over that feast the Anderson family and their friends all talked about their holiday highlights and most memorable adventures.

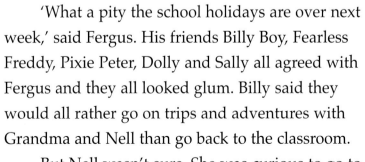

'What a pity the school holidays are over next week,' said Fergus. His friends Billy Boy, Fearless Freddy, Pixie Peter, Dolly and Sally all agreed with Fergus and they all looked glum. Billy said they would all rather go on trips and adventures with Grandma and Nell than go back to the classroom.

But Nell wasn't sure. She was curious to go to

an Australian school and learn about this new land and the interesting Australians as well as the rainforests and the Great Barrier Reef.

Nell had great respect for her teacher, Miss Murray, back in Scotland and she looked forward to meeting her new Australian teachers.

Nell's Father was working on the Reef Marine Park and Mother and Grandma were both working to earn money in the local fish restaurant by helping the chef to make fish feasts for overseas tourists. Nell felt she would need to learn and work at school to become a marine biologist.

Jan said he wished he could go to the school with his new friends. But he promised that after he returned home to Alice Springs he would write to his friends in Queensland.

'Why is it called Queensland?' asked Jan.

Fergus explained that it was England's Queen Victoria in the nineteenth century who wanted the state called after her. Jan shook his head and said,

Should auld acquaintance be forgot, and never brought to mind

'I think it should be called Sunnyland.'

Everyone cheered and started singing the Waltzing Matilda song:

'Once a jolly swagman camped by a billabong,

Under the shade of a coolabah tree;

And he sang as he watched and waited while his billy boiled,

Who'll come a-waltzing, Matilda, with me?'

After they all finished singing, the Crew of Three and their friends, as well as Grandma, Mr Mac and Frau Hesterberg, all promised to send each other letters and cards at Christmas and birthdays. Then they all cheered Grandma and Mr Mac and sang the Scottish farewell song, 'Auld Lang Syne'.

That night Nell opened her log-book and wrote of her adventures and new friends for Grandpa back in Scotland to read.

Should auld acquaintance be forgot, and auld lang syne!

Tom & Friends

Miss Murray

Grandmother

Grandfather

Mother May

Nell & Snowy

Father Jack

Frau Hesterberg

Jan

Rachel

Janet

Cap

Nell's Journey to Australia...

OBAN

SOUTHAMPTON

MADEIRA

TORTOLA

ANTIGUA

HONOLULU

PANAMA CANAL

Equator

N

W

E

S

AUSTRALIA

SYDNEY

YASAWA I-RARA

Nell and
The Old Man
of the Seas

Child of the Wind